California Gold Rush Fever

Bob Schaller

Baker Books

A Division of Baker Book House Co
Grand Rapids, Michigan 49516

Books in the X-Country Adventure series

Message in Montana
South Dakota Treaty Search
Adventure in Wyoming
Crime in a Colorado Cave
Mystery in Massachusetts
Treasure in Texas

© 2002 by Bob Schaller

Published by Baker Books
a division of Baker Book House Company
P.O. Box 6287, Grand Rapids, MI 49516-6287

Printed in the United States of America

Library of Congress Cataloging-in-Publication Data

Schaller, Bob.
    California gold rush fever / Bob Schaller.
        p.   cm. (X-country adventures; 7)
    Summary: While on vacation in California, Adam and Ashley and their parents learn about the time of the gold rush in that state and help try to recover a stolen antique saw blade that came from John Sutter's mill.
    ISBN 0-8010-4493-6
    [1. California—History—1846–1850—Juvenile fiction. 2. Sutter, John Augustus, 1803–1880—Juvenile fiction. [1. California—History—1846–1850—Fiction. 2. Sutter, John Augustus, 1803–1880—Fiction. 3. Brothers and sisters—Fiction. 4. Vacations—Fiction. 5. Mystery and detective stories.] I. Title
    PZ7.S33366 Cal 2002
    [Fic]—dc21   2001052893

For current information about all releases from Baker Book House, visit our web site:

http://www.bakerbooks.com

Contents

Gold Rush Girl

"If I knew it was there, sparkling beneath the surface, waiting for me," said Ashley Arlington from center stage, "then I would stay. But I do not know for certain. Therefore I must abandon the group and begin the long trip home to the East."

"How can you abandon us now?" a boy in a cowboy hat and jeans demanded of her. "We've finally made it to one of the most exciting places in this young country—at possibly one of the most exciting times in history!"

The group peered at her, waiting to see what this young woman would do next. She had astounded them all with her courage on the trip west, and now she seemed ready to throw away all her efforts and again brave the journey from coast to coast, this time to go back East alone, home.

"Are you sure?" Daisy, a girl in a long, blue dress, asked her. "We won't be going with you . . ."

"I know. I don't expect you to, but the news from home is worrisome. I will stay one more day, and if we still find nothing notable, I *must* go home to my family. Father is not well himself, and he has been taking care of poor Mother in my absence. The physical and financial stress is slowly killing him," Ashley explained to the group, tossing her long, blond hair behind her with a heavy sigh. Her blue eyes flashed as she looked into the distance. "We live for our dreams but also for those we carry in our hearts. Whether there is gold sparkling below these waters or not cannot matter against the luster of love in my heart for my parents."

As the curtain closed for a scene change, the audience clapped enthusiastically.

"Man, Ashley can really act, can't she?" Adam whispered to his mother.

Anne Arlington nodded in agreement. "All the young people in this production are very talented," she whispered back. "It also helps that the man who wrote the play did an outstanding job making this into a great story!"

The Arlington family was on vacation from their home in Washington, D.C. Ashley, seventeen, and Adam, sixteen, were enjoying their time in California, particularly their activities in the Bay Area. While the teens' father, Alex, was attending a conference in San Francisco, Adam and his mother did some sightseeing, enjoying a cable car ride and spending time at Fisherman's Wharf. Ashley was involved in a workshop on theater acting.

The play, *California Gold Rush Girl,* was the culmination of the two-day event, and it was written by the workshop director, a local high school drama instructor. Mrs. Arlington, a college history professor back in D.C., was pleased that Ashley had earned the starring role in the drama about the lives of the "gold bugs" or "'49ers" who rushed out to California to cash in on the Gold Rush in the 1800s. Learning from historical events had been an important part of the Arlington family's activities ever since the kids had been old enough to listen to bedtime stories about everyone from gold prospectors to presidents.

The curtain reopened, with Ashley and her cast mates standing in the middle of an onstage "stream" with washpans in their hands. Gold Rush Girl would not have to abandon the group quite so quickly—she could send word to her ailing mother and father that their fortune was won and their troubles were over, for her group had found gold!

"Stay and we could make enough money to maybe even start our own town," the boy in the cowboy hat said to her. "Send for your parents to come here—there aren't enough purty females in this golden country to even think about settling it when the gold pans out," he told her with a pleading face.

"It pains me to part with you," Ashley said, blushing and looking away from the boy. "But I already have more than I need to make a better life for my family. Settling this country will be important, but my parents aren't well enough to stand the trip here, and I had best return to them now rather than stay and be taken over by greed— or something else," she said wistfully as she once again met the cowboy's pleading eyes. "I bid you all farewell."

Ashley picked up her store of gold nuggets, waved to her partners, and walked determinedly off the stage. The lights faded as the other characters continued to mine for gold. The curtains drew closed for the final time, then the cast came out and took their bows.

"Thanks to every cast member who put forth so much effort," said Robert Hanson, the director. "I've never had a group who worked harder than this one. They had a good spirit of teamwork, with no one trying to outshine anyone else. A talented 'star' often shines at the expense of others, but not in this production," he said, casting an approving glance at Ashley. "Everyone sacrificed to make each character important and believable."

Mr. and Mrs. Arlington and Adam sat with the other families who had young people in the play. They listened as Mr. Hanson talked about his motivation for writing the play. He had always been fascinated by the Gold Rush, he said, especially the very few women characters who came to the by-and-large male prospector camps. The camps had names like Devil's Retreat and Gouge Eye, and they weren't safe places for women. Yet Mr. Hanson had an ancestor who had made her way to California during that exciting time, seeking to provide for ailing parents back East. He had based some of his play on her experiences.

"Colonel John Sutter went to the legendary General William Tecumseh Sherman's office in 1848 after discovering gold in Coloma, a town in which he had hoped to build a prosperous sawmill," Hanson told the audience. "Sutter and his group weren't necessarily thrilled about the discovery of gold—no longer could good help for reasonable pay be found—everyone was soon walking off the job to prospect for gold," he said. "Then the area was overrun with miners hoping to cash in.

"I found General Sherman's memoirs in which he wrote about Sutter's sawmill plans and how gold was suddenly discovered," Hanson continued. "The Gold Rush was a boon for some and a dilemma for others like John Sutter.

Two pieces of the old equipment from his sawmill exist today, in fact. One is here at the museum down by the pier. The other is in southern California somewhere, I think, in or near Antelope Valley."

"Antelope Valley!" Adam exclaimed to his parents. "We'll be there tonight!"

Mr. Arlington raised his hand. "Do you know where?" he asked Mr. Hanson. "We're heading down to Palmdale this afternoon, and we don't have time to stop by the museum here. We'd love to see the sawmill piece there."

It was almost 2 P.M., and the Arlingtons were planning to drive south to Palmdale in the Antelope Valley because a local college in that city was hosting a sports camp that Ashley and Adam were going to attend on Friday and Saturday. The kids excelled in sports at Thomas Jefferson High School in Washington, D.C., and they had both been chosen to try out for all-star teams at the camp. Ashley was going to participate in volleyball, while Adam would try out for the soccer team.

Mr. Hanson looked through his notes. "I don't believe that piece is on display," he informed them, "but I do have a contact number for an elderly woman who inherited the sawmill equipment from a relative. She is a descendant of the Sutter family."

"That would help us," Mrs. Arlington spoke up. "We'll try to contact her. We have several vacation days left; maybe we can arrange to see the piece."

"I would encourage you to do that," said Hanson. "The replica you saw onstage is not exact, but it's based on the piece at the museum here. There is a web site you can visit to see an old picture of the piece in Antelope Valley, though. I'll jot it down for you. And read the papers in the folder I gave out during the workshop if you'd like to learn more about John Sutter and General Sherman."

Ashley had joined her family from backstage by then and told them she had the folder in her backpack. She suggested they all read the information later that night.

After thanking the workshop director and exchanging e-mail addresses with some new friends she had made, Ashley headed out to the car with her family for the trip to southern California. They had to skip the dinner the theater cast was having to make the trip, but Ashley didn't complain. She knew that she and Adam needed a good night's rest before the following day's tryouts.

Mrs. Arlington, trim and blond like her kids, was an avid runner. She taught them—and her lawyer husband—the importance of good rest, food, and exercise to stay in shape. The family often started their days running, biking, or swimming together even on vacation, and they made sure to eat right and be well rested, especially when their travels involved activities like sports camps for the kids.

"In the car, gang," Mrs. Arlington urged her family. "You'll need to be wide awake for those practice games tomorrow, so let's get this trip over with."

"Hope our hotel has a pool," Adam commented as his dad started their SUV and pulled out of the parking lot. "I had to sit through this long historical play, and now I have to sit through this drive," he grumbled, giving Ashley a playful shove across the backseat. She scowled at him.

"I'm just kidding, Sis," he said. "You were terrific, and the play wasn't even too boring. What I really want to know, though, is if your cowboy friend will forget you forever in his greedy fever for gold, or if he's going to follow you back East to win your love and your hand in marriage?"

Sherman's Story

Ashley scowled at Adam again and gave him her own not-so-playful shove.

Mrs. Arlington turned around and eyed the two teens. "Yes, Adam, our hotel does have a pool, and I think both of you should cool off in it the instant we get there!"

"Okay, okay, I was just teasing her," Adam told his mom. "And you really did do a great job as Gold Rush Girl," he told Ashley with a grin.

"Thanks, Adam. I guess I'm just overtired from all the excitement today and nervous about tomorrow. I could use a few laps across the pool anyway when we get there!"

Ashley would trade in her long dress from the play for her volleyball uniform the following day. She was one of the best volleyball players on her school team, so it was no surprise that she had been selected to try out for the all-star team, which would showcase the top twenty players from the three hundred at camp. Adam's selection for the all-star soccer team tryouts was a bit more of a surprise, as he pointed out on the drive down the coast. Mr. Arlington had pulled off the highway, and the family was watching the surfers at Big Sur as they discussed the next day's tryouts.

"I'm glad my school coaches picked me," Adam said. "But I'm not the best player on our TJHS team."

Mr. Arlington had talked to the school coaches because he too had been pleasantly surprised that Adam had been chosen.

"The coaches said you were one of the hardest workers on the team—that you never slacked off on drills, even when it was late in the day," he told his son. "I was told that you finished near the front in all of the sprints and that you worked hard in all of your team activities. While you didn't personally score any goals, you did pass the ball to other players who made the goals. So you did help set up the goals. And that is certainly an important role on any team. You can't have five guys out there who just score and have no one setting them up for the goals!"

"Good point, Dad," Ashley said. Adam smiled as she punched him in the arm. "I know I couldn't have any kills from spiking the volleyball if I didn't have a good setter who set me up for the spikes," she added. "Wow! Look at that huge wave," she observed, pointing out the window.

"It's too bad we can't stay here longer, but we should get moving again," said Mr. Arlington as he pulled back onto the highway.

Mrs. Arlington turned toward the backseat.

"Do you have those papers Mr. Hanson talked about?" she asked Ashley. "They sounded intriguing."

"They're right here," Ashley answered. "If everybody can hear me, I'll read some of them."

"Go ahead," Mr. Arlington replied from the driver's seat.

The top of the first paper Ashley pulled out said that in chapter two of his memoirs, General Sherman wrote about touring the gold fields and meeting with several groups including John Sutter, the Mormons (at Mormon Island), and Kit Carson. Ashley read aloud:

I remember one day, in the spring of 1848, that two men, Americans, came into the office. They had just come down from Captain John Sutter on a special assignment. They wanted to see Governor Mason in person. I took them in to the colonel and left them together. After some time the colonel called me. I went in, and my attention was directed to a series of papers unfolded on his table, in which lay about half an ounce of placer-gold. Mason said to me, "What is that?"

Examining the larger pieces, I asked, "Is it gold?" He then asked me if I had ever seen native gold. "In 1844, in Upper Georgia, I saw some native gold," I replied, "but it was much finer than this, and it was in phials. If this is gold, though," I said to him, "it could be easily tested, first by its malleability, and next by acids."

I took a piece in my teeth; the metallic luster was perfect. I then called to the clerk, Baden, to bring an ax and hatchet from the backyard. I beat the largest piece out flat, and beyond doubt it was metal, and a pure metal!

"Wow!" Adam exclaimed. "Imagine the excitement!" Ashley continued reading Sherman's account:

Colonel Mason then handed me a letter from Captain Sutter stating he was building a sawmill at Coloma, forty miles up the American Fork, above his fort at New Helvitia. Sutter had already incurred considerable expense in this operation and he wanted a "preemption" to the quarter-section of land on which his mill sat, embracing the tailrace in which this particular gold had been found.

Mason instructed me to prepare a letter for Sutter in which I recited that California was yet a Mexican province, simply held by United States conquest. No U.S. laws yet applied to it, much less any land laws, which could only apply after a public survey. Therefore it was impossible to promise him title to the land; yet, as there were no settlements within forty miles of him, he was not likely to be disturbed by trespassers.

Mason signed my letter, handed it to one of Sutter's men who had brought the sample, and they departed.

"So the American settlers in California were literally out of their own country," Mrs. Arlington pointed out. "On the West Coast they were about as far away from the governing body of the U.S. as they could get—no wonder when the gold fever really rose, the mining camps set up their own forms of rough justice. There were no lawyers like your dad to see that things were done fairly and 'by the book.'"

"The conquest of California was over by then but not yet official?" asked Ashley. "Is that why Sutter couldn't get his title to the sawmill land?"

"Right," said Mr. Arlington this time. "And that's also why criminals didn't always get a trial by jury."

"Not the time to be a suspect in a crime!" said Adam.

"No, but still an exciting time to be alive," said his mother. "That gold discovered in the Sierra Nevada started a second sort of revolution in this country—it affected the whole world as the young United States uncovered a wealth of gold. And it populated California with bold, adventuresome settlers—just the sort needed to settle a new U.S. territory. Did you know that half a billion dollars' worth was taken out of the ground in less than a decade? It more than doubled the world's supply of gold."

"Amazing," Ashley said. "I'd really like to see the piece of equipment from Sutter's Mill where it all started. Do you think we can?"

"I still have the information Mr. Hanson gave us about Sutter's descendant, a Mrs. Esther Edwards," Mrs. Arlington said, pulling a scrap of paper out of her purse. "There's no number here, but it says 'Lancaster,' and that's the city just north of Palmdale—actually the two cities are basically connected to each other, though separate. I think we should try to look her up while we're in the area."

After a 370-mile drive, the Arlingtons arrived in Palmdale. At the hotel, the teens asked if they could take a walk.

"What about that pool?" Mrs. Arlington suggested. "It's quite late for the two of you to be walking around in a place we're not familiar with."

"I'd rather stretch out and get some fresh air after the long ride," Adam said. "I'll hit the pool in the morning. Maybe you and Dad could go with us?"

"That does sound good," Mr. Arlington spoke up.

After a brisk walk of several blocks, the family felt refreshed. They bought some bottled water and fruit to snack on and headed back to the hotel. Mr. and Mrs. Arlington turned in. Their bedroom was upstairs in their small suite, while Adam and Ashley would sleep downstairs.

"Great!" Adam said to his sister. "It won't bother Mom and Dad if I log on and do some surfing on the Internet before bed. Will it bother you to keep the light on a while?"

"What for?" Ashley said sleepily. "We have tryouts tomorrow!" She knew that her brother, once on the computer, might stay on for hours. Aside from excelling in sports at TJHS, Adam was also the computer whiz of the family. He often researched their trips and tourist destinations before they left home, and once they were on the road, he could find directions and information to help them on their way. His laptop traveled wherever he did.

"I just want to see if this Mrs. Edwards is in a database," he said. "I promise that's all. What was her first name?"

"Esther," Ashley told him with a sigh as she started getting ready for bed.

"I have it! Here's a number for her," Adam called out while she was brushing her teeth in the other room.

"Good work, but too late—at least for tonight. Remember, Adam, she's elderly. I don't think 10:30 P.M. is a good time to be calling her," Ashley pointed out.

"I know. I want to get to sleep anyway—maybe I can make a goal of my own tomorrow," he said, yawning. "We can try calling her tomorrow. She might set something up for us to see that piece of the sawmill."

With that thought, the teens turned out the light.

"Thanks for keeping your promise," Ashley said.

"*What* promise?" he asked. "I never promised you anything!"

"Yes, you did. You said you'd only look up that one thing on Mrs. Edwards, then you'd log off for tonight—and you actually stuck to it!"

Adam laughed. "I guess you're right—10:30 may be late for Mrs. Edwards, but it *is* pretty early for me to be off the laptop. But I can make up for it tomorrow night after our tryouts are over . . ."

Ashley groaned, then drifted off to sleep.

A Loss and a Win

Ashley and Adam couldn't believe it was already 8:00 when they woke up the day of the tryout games.

"Here's a note," Ashley said. "Mom and Dad already beat us down to the pool."

"Let's go," Adam urged.

The Arlington teens changed into swimsuits, grabbed their towels, and headed to the hotel's pool for a morning workout. Mr. and Mrs. Arlington met them poolside.

"Want to race, Dad?" Ashley challenged.

"Some other time," Mr. Arlington replied. "Your mother and I have already raced this morning."

Mrs. Arlington laughed. "He's not up to another match, Ashley. I put him in his place once already today."

The kids laughed at that. While not out of shape, Mr. Arlington wasn't the fitness fanatic that his wife was, and clearly Ashley and Adam took after her. Mr. Arlington sometimes had all he could do to keep up with his family's exercise schedule, though he admitted that his work as a lawyer didn't keep him in shape all by itself. He knew it was important for him to stay physically active outside his workplace, but he'd already had enough for one day racing his wife across the pool.

After loosening up in the water, the kids joined their parents in the hotel dining room and ordered bagels, fruit, and juice. Back in their suite they packed their gear for the tryout games and checked the weather on TV.

"No rain for today. It should be perfect for our games," Adam said.

"We'd better head out," Mr. Arlington told them.

"Can we call Esther Edwards first?" Ashley asked. "Adam found her number on the Internet last night."

Mr. and Mrs. Arlington exchanged looks. They had already talked about contacting her and had decided to go ahead, but they weren't sure if they should let one of the kids make the call. Since Ashley had asked, though, they decided to let her give it a try.

"Remember, Mr. Hanson said she's elderly. She may take some time to answer the phone. And she may not want to talk to a stranger, Ashley," said Mr. Arlington. "If she seems hesitant, continue to be polite, and perhaps let your mother or me talk to her."

"Right, Dad," Ashley said as she dialed the number Adam gave her.

The phone rang three times, then it was picked up.

"Hello?" said a pleasant voice.

"Hi. My name is Ashley Arlington, and I'm looking for Mrs. Esther Edwards," Ashley said in her most polite tone.

"I am Mrs. Edwards," the voice said. "May I help you with something?"

"I hope so, Mrs. Edwards," Ashley said. "I was in a theater workshop in San Francisco, and we did a play involving the Gold Rush that started at John Sutter's sawmill in the 1800s."

"Why, that must have been *Gold Rush Girl!*" Mrs. Edwards interrupted. "I have a friend there whose granddaughter, Sarah Jenkins, was performing in the play. My friend told me all about it because she knows I'm a descendant of John Sutter. I believe she even gave my name to the workshop director."

"That's right!" Ashley said excitedly. "We got your name from Mr. Hanson, the director, and Sarah and I became good friends at the workshop."

"How lovely, dear," Mrs. Edwards said. "I'm pleased to hear it. What can I do for you?"

"Well, Mr. Hanson told us you might have one of the two original pieces of the sawmill left. We didn't have time to see the one in the museum there after the play, and we hoped—my parents, my brother, Adam, and I—that we could visit you while we're in the area and actually see the sawmill, maybe get a picture with you in it, if that would be permissible."

"Certainly, my dear," Mrs. Edwards said. "It's so good to talk to a young person who takes an interest in history. That's a rare thing these days!"

"Actually, my mom is a history professor back home in Washington, D.C.," Ashley said. "But my brother and I would still like historical things even if she wasn't."

"Good for you!" said Mrs. Edwards. "Now may I talk to that history professor, and we'll make some arrangements to meet?"

Ashley politely said good-bye and handed the phone to her mother.

"Mrs. Edwards? This is Ashley's mother, Anne Arlington. My husband, Alex, and I would be very grateful if we could bring the kids to see your piece of history."

"Lovely, Professor Arlington! It's so refreshing to find a family interested in what we eighty-year-olds have to say. My great-uncle was actually one of the more experienced men on John Sutter's sawmill crew. I have a few stories about him we could share."

"Please, call me Anne," said Mrs. Arlington, "and I'd love to hear those stories."

"All right, Professor Anne. I'm a widow now, so I live alone out here in Lancaster. Where are you coming from?" Mrs. Edwards asked.

"Just down the road in Palmdale," Mrs. Arlington answered. "The kids are at a sports camp here at the college today and tomorrow, but after that we're free."

"You have talented children to be in theater and sports. You must be very proud of them," said Mrs. Edwards. "I can't wait to meet them. And we're only about twenty-five minutes down the road. What would you think of coming over Monday? You see, I'd like to have you visit then because there are some geologists coming who want to see if there is a residue from the lumber on the old sawmill blade. There are also some members of the California Historical Society joining us, and a history professor and her interested family would make the day complete. The media is even coming, and I'm making cookies and refreshments, too. This is more excitement over an old piece of equipment than I've seen in years!"

"Wonderful," Mrs. Arlington said. "We'd love to come be part of the excitement. What should we bring?"

"Just yourselves, dear," Mrs. Edwards answered. "I'm so grateful for your interest. Who knows why my piece of history wasn't presented to a museum long ago, but my father's brother, another uncle, passed it along to me when he died forty years ago. My husband and I put it into storage without realizing its worth.

"When my husband passed away—we have no children, you see—I decided to settle his estate and take everything out of storage. I've only taken the cover off the old mill piece once, just recently—I had practically forgotten it was there. I called the historical society, and they filled me in on some documentation they uncovered stating that there might be something in this equipment that was overlooked in the past. Naturally, they checked out the piece in the San Francisco museum already, but they didn't find anything. You can imagine their excitement when they got my call! They even wanted to send an armed guard over when they found out what I had. Well, I wouldn't have any part of that, but I told them they could come over on Monday themselves, and they still insist on bringing the local police along in case they find something priceless. I don't know if their information is old folklore or factual, but they aim to find out, and so do I."

"Thank you for including us in all of this," Mrs. Arlington told the elderly woman after jotting down directions to her house, which was off a dirt road just north of Lancaster before the city of Rosamond. "Thank you for speaking so kindly with our daughter, too. She and our son, Adam, are looking forward to meeting you on Monday."

After hanging up the phone, Mrs. Arlington told her husband and kids what Mrs. Edwards had said about the possibility of something being contained either within or as part of the old sawmill equipment.

"If the U.S. Geological Survey and the California Historical Society members want to be in on this, it must be pretty special," Adam said. "We're lucky we get to be there when they search for whatever it is they're after."

"It sure would be exciting to see what they find," he added. "Right now I'd settle just for knowing what it is they're looking for."

"Sounds like Mrs. Edwards didn't know herself," Mrs. Arlington commented, "so no help there. We'll have to wait till Monday. It could be something factual, or just folklore like she said. We'll find out Monday either way. Right now, let's get over to the college for the tryouts."

While Mrs. Arlington checked out the college's history department, Mr. Arlington watched both Adam and Ashley compete against the other camp attendees in tryout games. To everyone's surprise, the siblings were picked for their respective all-star teams.

The next day they headed back to Antelope Valley College for Ashley's game in the college gym. Ashley played a good match, but her team was trounced, losing what was supposed to be a five-set match in just three games, 15–3, 15–7, 15–10. Ashley had several good spikes, but she didn't have many opportunities because her team members weren't helping set each other up. Although the other team's girls weren't as tall as those on Ashley's team, it didn't make any difference because they were in sync the entire match, whereas Ashley's team seemed to lack teamwork. It was a frustrating situation but a good lesson.

The Arlingtons moved outside and had lunch on a blanket after Ashley had showered and changed.

"I haven't been in a game with a loss that lopsided in a long time," she said. "It makes me appreciate my teammates back home. Even when TJHS plays better teams, we don't usually get beaten like that."

"Well, the scores got closer each game at least," Mr. Arlington pointed out. "But I noticed some other things the team was doing—or wasn't doing—that seemed to make the difference. Do you know what I'm talking about?" he asked Ashley.

"Do I!" she answered. "Do you mean the problem with teamwork? I felt like no one was helping anyone else on our team; everybody was trying for the glory shots. When I played out front, only a couple girls helped set me up for spikes. It was a little disappointing."

"That was it," her dad agreed. "The lack of teamwork really hurt your side, though it did get better as the games went on. But not good enough to pull off any wins."

"We had a lot more height than they did, but even that didn't help. Just goes to show that a smaller team can be better if they do the fundamentals—and the teamwork— better. I think it's hard for some kids to remember that being an 'all-star' player doesn't mean trying to be a star playing all by yourself and forgetting about the rest of the team."

"Good lesson to learn, and I can see you know that already because of the way you display teamwork in your matches at school," Mrs. Arlington said. "But that's what sports are all about really, teaching us lessons about life, right?"

A half-hour later Adam played in his soccer game. Although Adam himself claimed that he wasn't one of the better players, he looked it in this game. He set up five of his team's eight goals in an 8–7 win. When the tournament's MVP award was announced, though, it went to a boy from the other team who scored six of their goals.

Adam's coach had lobbied the officials to make Adam the MVP. "Sorry you didn't get it," he told Adam. "You were definitely our team's MVP today, though. I promise you that!"

Adam smiled and held up the trophy all the kids on the winning team had received.

"It's okay, coach. I'd rather have the team win than the MVP glory. We won the championship, and I'd much rather have this trophy than that plaque. Plus, I got so much better at the game and learned so much in two days—where to be, what to look for. I got way more out of this camp than I ever hoped for. I'm not even a top ten player back home. I'm not even a starter, and I played junior varsity last year."

"If talent like yours is on their bench, I'd love to coach that team on the field," the coach said, smiling and shaking hands with Adam and his family. "I have a feeling, though, that you're not going to be a benchwarmer this next season!" he said as he walked away.

The Arlingtons went out to dinner and did some shopping, then drove back to their hotel. In the suite, the message light was blinking. That wasn't unusual, as Mr. and Mrs. Arlington had business calls coming in even on vacation. But this was Saturday night, and the message was no business call.

"Oh, how horrible!" Mrs. Arlington exclaimed as she listened to the message. "Mrs. Edwards has had some trouble. The sawmill relic was stolen from her garage either late last night or early this morning! I guess she needed that armed guard after all—she called the police, but it's gone!"

The Saw Blade Burglary

"Gone?" Ashley asked with a look that was equal parts disappointment and disbelief. "But it can't be . . . poor Mrs. Edwards!"

Mrs. Arlington motioned to her husband. "Do you think we could head out to her house if we called ahead and asked if it's all right?" she asked him.

"Great idea," he said. "You mentioned she doesn't have any children or relatives in the area. She might need someone to lean on besides the police officers."

"That would be nice to do," said Ashley. "We'll get ready while Mom calls in case she says yes."

"Wait a minute," her father said. "You two kids have got to be tired from your games, and I'm sure Mrs. Edwards is tired, too—she's so elderly and has been through a lot. Maybe just your mother and I should go over while you two stay here. You can order a pizza, watch a movie, and recover from your tournaments. It is a crime scene, after all. The fewer people there the better, I think."

"Oh, Alex, you may be the best lawyer in D.C., but think about who has solved most of the mysteries we've run into so far," Mrs. Arlington reminded her husband. She had hung up the phone and overheard his comments. "It wasn't you or I that always had all the important insights—and these two have shown that they can handle themselves in this kind of situation before."

"All right, Mom!" Adam cried. "So can we go?"

"Let's go, then," Mr. Arlington gave in. "I can't argue against your character witness for these two, Anne!"

Everyone laughed.

"Thanks, Dad," Adam said. "I promise we won't trample any evidence like footprints and stuff, and we'll be really quiet and polite."

"Right," Mr. Arlington said. "Just let the police do their job—we've talked about that before. You two supersleuths don't have your badges yet, you know."

The Arlingtons made the trip to Mrs. Edwards's house in less than a half hour. They pulled onto her dirt road and couldn't see any lights at first, but a half mile down they could see a house lit up like a candle. There was a police car and a county sheriff's SUV in the driveway.

The house was old but well kept up. It was a long, one-story dwelling with dark shingles and gray sides that looked freshly painted. The garage was detached from the house, maybe twenty yards away. It had a weather vane on top. An old water pump with a handle sat in front of the house. Adam speculated that it too was an antique and probably wasn't operable anymore.

The Arlingtons parked their SUV out of the way of the police vehicles, careful to leave it where it wouldn't block any cars in or prevent other emergency response vehicles from entering. They got out and were greeted by a police officer.

Detective Steven Simon introduced himself to the family. "Is Mrs. Edwards expecting you?" he asked. "There's been some trouble here, and she's quite distraught. This might not be the best time for unexpected guests."

"Yes, sir," Mr. Arlington told Detective Simon. "We just talked to her by phone half an hour ago, and she asked us to come on over. We tried to stay to the side of the road so we wouldn't cover up any tire tracks or other clues you folks might be searching for."

"That was thoughtful, but you don't need to worry about that at this point," said the detective. "This happened about six hours ago, so we've done pretty much all we need to do. The big part of the crime scene is over in the driveway in front of the garage, and we've gone over every inch of it. All that's left is to sit down with Mrs. Edwards and wrap this up."

At that moment Mrs. Edwards came out and met the Arlingtons.

"I'm so sorry you kids came all the way out here when there's no longer any sawmill relic or anything to see," she said.

"Hey, that's not true—we're getting to meet you," Ashley said, shaking the woman's hand gently.

"Well, bless your heart," Mrs. Edwards responded.

Detective Simon extended his arm, and Mrs. Edwards grabbed hold of it. He walked her into the garage, his big flashlight illuminating the path ahead of them.

"So someone actually stole the entire sawmill?" Adam asked. "That's a huge task. Earlier I searched online for 'antique sawmills' and saw a picture of one. Those things had to be really heavy."

The detective laughed. "No, they didn't take the whole thing," he said. "But what they did take was still very heavy. It was the main saw blade encased in a cast-iron shell. I imagine the thing weighed at least 150 pounds."

Mr. Arlington looked at his wife in surprise.

"Just the saw blade?" he asked Simon. "That's odd, isn't it?"

Simon shined his light toward the garage. The big door was open. It looked like an antique store inside, with old lamps, a wood-burning stove, and other tools and furniture scattered about. All of it was heavily covered in dust.

"Let's go into the house, please, because just looking in here right now, knowing those thieves stole my antique mill equipment, makes me feel sick to my stomach," Mrs. Edwards said.

"Of course," Detective Simon agreed.

On the way over to the house, the city police officer spoke briefly to Simon and bid Mrs. Edwards good evening.

"You're in good hands with Detective Simon here," the officer said to her. "This is a county matter for the sheriff's department anyway because of where you are located, but I'm glad I was nearby and could respond to make sure you weren't hurt."

"Just my pride is hurt," Mrs. Edwards said, smiling tiredly. "The rest of me is fine, but I appreciate your quick response."

"It was nice to meet you, ma'am, and I wish you speedy recovery of your goods. I'll leave you in Detective Simon's capable hands now." With that, he got in his cruiser and drove away.

Everyone went into the house, and Mrs. Edwards led them into the living room, which was filled with more antiques. These were sparkling clean and had been kept up well. The furniture was like something Adam and Ashley had seen before.

"This reminds me of Great-grandma's house," Adam said quietly to Ashley. "The flower pattern on the couch and its shape, that's kind of like what Great-grandma has."

Ashley nodded. Even the lamps were old and charming.

"Here, everyone, have a seat," Mrs. Edwards invited. "I have some cookies and milk if you'd like."

"I'm sure the kids would love that," replied Mrs. Arlington. "Alex and I would just like some water, if that would be all right."

"Of course. Just go out front and pump it yourself—you saw the water pump as you came in, didn't you?" Mrs. Edwards asked.

That caught everyone's attention.

"There was a lot of rust on that thing," Adam whispered to his mother, "so maybe you should go with the milk."

"Oh, heavens, I'm just pulling a prank on you," Mrs. Edwards said, a big smile across her face. Detective Simon laughed heartily. "There's plenty of ice-cold water in the kitchen," she finished.

"Let me help you," Mrs. Arlington said, getting up off the couch. "You've already had a hard day."

In the kitchen, Mrs. Edwards pulled out some glasses.

"These are astounding," Mrs. Arlington exclaimed, holding one up. They were of a printed design and looked to be very old.

"Been in the family for decades and decades," Mrs. Edwards said proudly, "though the set is no longer as complete as it used to be."

They took the snacks back into the living room. Detective Simon had his notebook open. He addressed Mrs. Edwards.

"If you would tell us about the sawmill and what happened, I'm just going to listen and see if I can pick up anything to add to what I already have here," he told her.

"Certainly," Mrs. Edwards said. "I was going through everything that we had moved—it took me a while. I had no idea what all of it was. I didn't even remember where all of it came from, but as you might have noticed in the garage, I have a hard time throwing things away."

Mrs. Arlington laughed. "I think the historical society is going to end up thanking you for that," she said. "Even if the sawmill isn't recovered, there are plenty of other items in your collection to interest them."

Mrs. Edwards smiled and pulled some papers from a binder. "Yes, I realize that now," she said. "I knew everything I had was antique and perhaps of some value, but 'of value' to me means very little in terms of money. It's all high in sentimental value, and to me that makes it priceless. When you get older, your memories are what you keep and hold close to your heart. All the things I have bring back some kind of memory, whether it's of someone I knew or a relative about whom I'd heard stories over the years. The gaps I just fill in with my imagination—like the director who wrote your Gold Rush play, dear," she said to Ashley.

She unfolded the half piece of paper from the binder. It was torn about halfway down. She held it up. "This is the one that has caused all the sensation," she said, carefully holding up the old piece of paper. "This is what all the fuss is about."

Questions without Answers

"This is a note passed down from my great-uncle Arnold Atkinson, who worked at John Sutter's sawmill. It's not long by any means, but its age makes it a bit hard to read."

Mrs. Edwards put on the glasses that hung around her neck and started to read aloud:

> This equipment can be kept in the family or sold. I know it seems very odd to pass along an entire sawmill down a generation or more. But the blade on this sawmill holds a lot of history in it. This was the blade we were using on some lumber we had brought in the day the gold was discovered. You can see from the huge gash and the missing teeth in the blade what happened. Maybe I'm simply a man who can't let go of some broken machinery, but there's such a story behind this sawmill—it started

something that spread across the entire country and was the making and taking of many lives.

We were working fourteen-hour days, exhausting ourselves in the race to provide new settlers with lumber for their buildings. Sutter always was one to see an opportunity and turn it into a business. I was just glad of the steady work his mill provided me in such an unsettled territory. We fed in this piece of lumber, and suddenly the saw blade came to a grinding halt. Look to the blade to see why. We all looked ourselves and were astonished...

The Arlingtons and Detective Simon were eager to hear why Atkinson had suddenly been astonished by what he saw.

Mrs. Edwards took off her reading glasses.

"That's where the note ends," she said. "The rest of it is nowhere to be found. I don't believe it was stolen; you can tell by the ripped edge that it happened years and years ago. But this does tell us that the sawmill blade has historical value. I called the college when I found this, and they referred me to the U.S. Geological Survey and the California Historical Society. Those folks were so kind. They called the media Friday and arranged the press conference and event that we were going to have on Monday. We were going to open the blade case together and see what secrets it might have held to astonish us."

She passed the paper to Ashley, who carefully held it flat while her parents and Adam examined it with her.

"Amazing," Adam said. "I wonder what it all means?"

Simon was writing some notes. "That's the question I'd like answered," he said. "That could provide quite a few clues about who stole the sawmill blade and why."

Mrs. Arlington gently took the paper from Ashley and handed it back to Mrs. Edwards.

"Esther, this note at least should be preserved. The story of Sutter's Mill is in every history textbook written about this country's settlement—this is an important piece of history all by itself."

"Yes, I know, dear. I'll put it in good hands at the historical society if they want it. I just wish I had more clues that would help recover the stolen equipment. I would so like to find out what my great-uncle was hinting at in this unfinished letter. It's incredible that this has been handed down through the years—I guess my family is just that way. But we've saved so many things that we just didn't always get around to tracking everything down, and now, when I realize what value this had, it seems too late . . ."

Adam had an idea.

"Even if it's too late for the sawmill, Mrs. Edwards—and we won't give up on that yet—it's not too late for your other antiques. Maybe you could log everything in the garage and house so you'd know what you have to pass along for the future. You know, like have these things appraised by the historical society or something so there would be a record of their history and value."

Mrs. Edwards smiled. "Of course, young man, that should have been done ages ago. But you get to growing the crops and living your life, and it gets overlooked. One thing I've learned already is not to overlook it any longer— I don't have relatives left to pass it down to. Most everyone in my family is gone, aside from a few out East. I don't know that this stuff would interest them, though. I think it belongs here in California where its history is, so I'm going to begin donating it to museums through the historical society so others can enjoy it. No more sitting in the garage gathering dust—or being stolen! Making a log of it would be just what's needed to get a start on that, I think."

Detective Simon put down his pen. "If you'd like, I could help you with that," he said. "I'll have to come back tomorrow or the next day to go through things again anyway. We could certainly create a list of the antiques you have."

Mrs. Edwards thanked him for his kind offer.

"Do you have any idea who might be behind this theft?" Mr. Arlington asked Detective Simon.

Simon flipped to a page in his notebook. "One guess is as good as another at this point," he told the Arlingtons. "We did hear from neighbors down the road that a green pickup truck with a red or orange tarp in the back was seen leaving the area just before sunup. That tarp could have been covering the blade case. We've notified the authorities to watch for the truck on the highways and interstates leaving this area.

"Another factor is that so few people knew about this, even after Mrs. Edwards made her calls. We're in contact with the media to find out just how far the word spread and to whom. But it was broadcast as local news, so that would open the suspect list to anyone who heard the report about the upcoming press conference concerning a possibly valuable historical relic. The intention was to have just a few media representatives, the historical society, and the geologists in on this, but someone goofed by letting it out to the general public ahead of time."

Mr. Arlington leaned forward. "Why would someone steal the mill blade?" he asked. "This isn't something they could put in a backpack or purse and take somewhere. It's a large item, and a cumbersome object as well. Certainly it would raise more questions for the thieves to show up with it than they could get answered anywhere."

Simon tapped his notebook with his pen.

"You'd think so," he commented. "We've alerted anyone we think the thieves might go to—antique dealers, hardware stores, and the like. This isn't a diamond blade or something worth hundreds of thousands of dollars. It's a damaged blade from a sawmill dating back 150 years, which gives it historical value but limits the thieves' options!"

Adam and Ashley cleaned up their places and then offered to take everyone's glasses to the kitchen.

"Thanks, you two," Mrs. Edwards said. "Just leave everything by the sink."

"Is there anything we can do to help?" Adam asked Detective Simon as they came back in and sat down.

"If you see a green pickup truck with a large object in back, you'd be my hero," he told Adam with a wry smile.

"Mine, too," Mrs. Edwards added, patting Adam's knee.

"But aside from that, I really don't know," Simon said. "Obviously the press conference isn't going to happen as planned. But since several folks came from out of town, we're still going to meet here Monday and put our heads together to see if we can come up with any theories, any ideas about the motivation behind this theft and who might be involved. If it's all right with Mrs. Edwards, you'd be welcome to come back and be part of that discussion.

A lawyer, a history professor, and two sharp kids might have some insights we'd appreciate."

"I'd welcome you all back," Mrs. Edwards told the Arlingtons, who stood and shook hands with her and Detective Simon.

Walking to their SUV on the dirt road, the Arlingtons wondered what had happened in that very spot this morning.

"She is so nice," Ashley said as they drove away. She shook her head. "I can't believe anyone would do anything bad to that sweet woman."

"That's how criminals are," Mr. Arlington said. "Selfish by nature. They don't care about how what they're doing affects anyone else—they're just in it for themselves. While what they do may seem like it takes daring, it's just the opposite—they're cowards. They don't want to do honest work to make a living. They want to take, take, take, and they hurt people like Mrs. Edwards in the process."

"Watch the road, Alex," Mrs. Arlington said, patting her husband on the back.

"Dad, are you upset over Mrs. Edwards, or is there a story behind this lecture?" Ashley asked with concern.

"Both," her dad answered. He turned off the radio and shook his head at what was apparently a none-too-pleasant memory.

"When your mother and I were on our honeymoon, someone broke into our hotel room while we were on the beach," he said. "I didn't really care that they got my credit cards and a hundred dollars. But I was livid that they took my whole wallet. There was a picture of my mother in there that I could never replace. The money and cards, those are replaceable. But the picture and some of your mother's clothes and things had sentimental value—those kinds of things can't be replaced."

"I'm just glad we left our wedding rings on when we went down to swim," Mrs. Arlington said. "I had thought about taking mine off in the room—it felt so new and strange, and I didn't want it to slip off in the water. . . ."

"Good thing you kept it on, Mom," Adam said. "Were those thieves ever caught?"

"No," his dad answered, "but we canceled the credit cards before the thieves took us to the cleaners with them, so all we lost in terms of money was the cash. It was a hassle, though, getting our driver's licenses, insurance cards, and all that other stuff replaced!"

The family got back to the hotel before the pool closed for the night, so they decided to do a few laps.

After they finished swimming, they went back to their hotel suite. Ashley put on a San Francisco 49ers sweatshirt she had bought a few days before and was drying her hair. She looked out the window and could hardly believe her eyes.

"Adam, get Dad," she hissed.

"What? Why?" he asked, walking toward Ashley. She waved him away with her hand behind her back.

She casually drew the curtain and switched off the light as if getting ready to turn in for the night.

"Just get Dad—now—please!" she urged. "Hurry!"

Green Truck Getaway

Adam rushed up the suite stairs to get his father, who had just put on his robe.

"Ash needs you downstairs—hurry!" Adam said.

"Is she okay? Did she get hurt?" Mr. Arlington asked.

"No. She just said to get you quick—I have no idea why."

Mr. Arlington came down the stairs with Mrs. Arlington right behind him. When they came into view, Ashley motioned again with her hand for her parents to stop.

"I might be way too tired and be assuming too much," Ashley said, "but in our hotel parking lot, behind where we parked and over two spaces, is a big, green pickup with something huge in the bed, covered with a tarp. I know it could be anything, or nothing of concern, but . . ."

Adam put on his shoes. "I'm going out to see what it is," he said.

Mr. Arlington put out his arm to catch his son. "What if those guys are keeping an eye on the truck? What if they have guns? What if it's not the right truck? I have Detective Simon's card; let's just give him a call," he urged.

Mr. Arlington spoke quickly with the detective.

"He suggested we keep an eye out the window, but to be smart about it," Mr. Arlington told his family. "He's sending a car right over to check it out."

As the family stood at the window, a blast of wind outside shook it. The same gust also blew the tarp off the truck bed. It came to rest on the ground behind the truck.

"It's a circular casing!" Adam said. "It looks just like Detective Simon and Mrs. Edwards described!"

Mr. Arlington picked up the phone and redialed Simon.

"Hi, Steve, it's Alex Arlington again," he said. "Hey, I don't want us to get ahead of ourselves, but we think this might be it. A gust of wind blew the tarp off the truck while we were looking out, and there's a big, round case in the truck's bed. It looks to be made of iron or something."

"The police are on the way," Simon said. "Can you see a license plate number from where you are?"

Mr. Arlington looked, shocked that he hadn't thought of it sooner. "Actually we can't see a plate on the front, and the truck is facing us," he informed Simon. "But it's definitely a Ford, maybe an older F-150."

"Okay, nice work. Keep an eye out—carefully," Simon said, then hung up.

Ashley pointed. "Look, someone's running toward the truck—now he's getting in!" she cried.

Mrs. Arlington closed the corner of the curtain where they had been peering out. "Careful, Ashley and Adam," she warned. "They haven't noticed us yet, and we don't want them to. It was smart of you to turn off the lights down here, but there are too many of us at this window. Alex, why don't you and Adam go upstairs, turn those lights off, and look out from up there? Ash and I will keep watching here—we'll all have a better view."

Mr. Arlington and Adam went running up the stairs in a sprint. Both pairs pulled their curtains back ever so slightly, so as not to be seen, and watched outside.

The man in the truck got out and threw a bag into the back, then he quickly retrieved the tarp from the ground and put it back over whatever was in the truck's bed.

Just then a second man came out holding a radio.

"It's a police scanner!" Mrs. Arlington said to Ashley. She walked to the stairs and called up, "Alex, can you see that? They have a police scanner!"

"I see it," he called back down. "That means they know the police are on the way, so they're hotfooting it out of here. Let's hope the police get here first!"

It hadn't even been two minutes since the Arlingtons called Detective Simon, and yet the green truck was already backing out on its way toward the road. There was little doubt now that the two men were up to no good, whether that involved the sawmill blade or something else. As the truck backed out of its parking space, Mr. Arlington slipped on some sweatpants and a sweatshirt.

"We'll go with you, Dad!" Ashley said.

"No way," their dad said. "I'm going to meet the police downstairs. You wait here in case you can spot something else happening or in case Detective Simon calls back."

Ashley and Adam protested, but their mother backed up her husband. "Only one of us needs to go, and it should be your dad," she confirmed. "Those men could be dangerous. Be careful, Alex," she added as he went out.

She and the kids peered out the window and noted the truck was going north on Avenue B, likely headed for the highway. She called that information in to Simon, who was already on his way to the hotel.

"I'll relay that information, then come down and see you folks," he told her. "I'm coming from the north side of town, and once they're off Avenue B, they'll drive toward the south or east side, I'd guess. I won't be able to intercept them. But I'll forward your info to the other patrol cars. See you in a few."

The kids and Mrs. Arlington watched as the police car pulled up outside. They saw Mr. Arlington identify himself and show his license. A second cruiser pulled in and parked, and behind that followed Detective Simon.

Mr. Arlington explained to the group what had taken place. "Can we go up to your room and talk?" the detective said quietly to Mr. Arlington. "We don't know if there are any accomplices who might still be here in the hotel. I think it might be safer if we talked somewhere other than where you might be seen with us."

"Right," agreed Mr. Arlington.

They headed into the lobby, where Mrs. Arlington and the kids had come down to meet them.

"Back upstairs, quick," Mr. Arlington said as he ushered his family a few feet back toward the elevators. On the way up he explained that for their own protection they shouldn't be seen with the police officers.

Once they were back in their room, a policewoman called from the hotel's front desk, where she had been talking to the clerk. The two men were apparently alone together, she informed Simon, and hadn't left anyone behind, but she and her partner would check the hotel thoroughly just to be sure.

Adam watched out the window as she and her partner looked over the area where the truck had been parked. She radioed up to Simon.

"This truck was carrying a lot of dirt on its tires, and probably underneath as well, because there's still some out here," she told him.

"As I suspected," he told her. "The reporting party, a Mrs. Edwards, lives out in the rural area north of Lancaster—all dirt roads. See if you can get some clues out there."

Simon turned his attention to the Arlingtons, and Ashley recounted how she had been looking out the window when she was shocked to see a green pickup truck.

"I was just looking to see how many stars were out, because it had been a beautiful night," Ashley explained. "I was looking around the parking lot, and I just happened to see this green truck under the light. I was so shocked, I couldn't say a word for a minute. I knew it fit the description you had given us at Mrs. Edwards's house."

The Arlingtons then combined what they remembered seeing to produce the best possible description of the two men they could. Both were white males in their late twenties or early thirties. The first one was tall, maybe 6'2" and slender, about 160 pounds. The second man was shorter, perhaps 5'5" or 5'6", but must have weighed at least 200 pounds, the Arlingtons all agreed.

Simon asked for facial descriptions, but none of the Arlingtons had seen the men well enough or long enough to be very accurate.

"The tall one was wearing a baseball cap backward," Ashley recalled. "The shorter, chubby one had a mustache—I think. He was wearing a knit cap, too, a black one, which I thought was odd because it's at least 60 degrees tonight."

"Actually, I heard it was 63 when I was on my way over, so you're close there," Simon said. "It would seem kind of odd for a man to be wearing what is usually a winter cap, but some people do that these days."

"Too bad these guys had a scanner," Adam said to Detective Simon, "otherwise you might have caught them."

"Hey, listen," Simon said, "that's a little disappointing, but we're pretty fortunate you were able to spot them and their truck in the very hotel you're staying at. Ashley, that was excellent observation on your part—really sharp! They and their truck are still in town, and among the four of you, you've given us a very strong description of these fellows. You've given us a lot to go on, where we had almost nothing before." Simon gave Adam a pat on the back. "You've already helped a ton!" he finished.

"It was pretty fortuitous that we went out to Mrs. Edwards's place tonight," Mrs. Arlington said, "or we'd have had these guys in the truck right under our noses all night and never would have had a clue."

Adam was still disgusted at the turn of events. "I can't believe we let them get away," he growled. "We should have done something to stop them!"

"Absolutely not, Adam!" Detective Simon protested. "Never put yourselves in the line of criminals even when you think you can handle a situation. For more than one citizen who got in the way of ruthless criminals in an attempt to help the police or be heroes, their first attempt was their last—if you get what I mean. So I mean *never*."

"Yes, sir," Adam said, embarrassed but still frustrated.

"Detective Simon is right," Mr. Arlington emphasized. "Think about it: Right after we called the police, those guys picked it up on the scanner. Thank goodness we called

Detective Simon and he called it in, otherwise those guys listening to their scanner would have known who at the hotel had turned them in. Had we gone out to the pickup truck after we called, we'd have run right into the thieves— or them into us. Remember how quickly they left here?"

"I know, Dad," Adam said. "We did the safe, smart thing. I just wish we could have done more."

"You did fine, son," Simon said. He again thanked the Arlington family, then he turned toward the door. "There are so many side roads around here that those guys could stay hidden a long time if things work out just right for them," he said on his way out. "At the same time, if we do catch them, I'll let you know first thing in the morning. If they're not apprehended, do you still plan to be at Mrs. Edwards's house for Monday's meeting?"

Mr. and Mrs. Arlington looked at their kids. The look in their eyes gave their parents the answer.

"I'd say it's a safe bet we'll be out there tomorrow," Mrs. Arlington said, grinning. "I think there are two kids here who wouldn't miss that for just about anything."

Adam and Mr. Arlington walked Simon to the hotel lobby. The phone started to ring as soon as they stepped out of the room. Mrs. Arlington picked it up.

"Hello, this is Anne Arlington," she said.

"Good evening, Professor Anne; sorry to call so late," a tired voice said. "This is Esther Edwards."

"Hello, Esther!" Mrs. Arlington said. "Well, do I have some news for you! I'm so glad you called."

"That's fine, dear," Mrs. Edwards replied. "But can I go first? I have some news that's going to change everything!"

The Lumber Link

Mrs. Arlington motioned toward Ashley.

"Mrs. Edwards, would it be all right if I had Ashley run upstairs and pick up the phone to listen in?" she asked. "I'd also like to have Ashley help me fill you in on what happened here tonight. Detective Simon just left."

"Detective Simon?" Mrs. Edwards repeated. "Okay, dear, maybe you better go first."

Mrs. Arlington and Ashley filled in the older woman on what had happened from the time that Ashley spotted the truck in the parking lot until all the excitement was over and the detective had gone home.

"So Detective Simon said they were about 99 percent certain that these are the guys and that it was the saw blade we spotted in the bed of the truck," Mrs. Arlington told her. "We saw the cast-iron case because the wind blew off the orange tarp they had covering it—apparently they hadn't thought to tie it down or didn't want to take the time. We're hoping the police will catch up with them tonight, but who knows what will happen?"

"There are so many back roads with nooks and crannies someone could drive down and hide in for a night or two," Mrs. Edwards sighed. "The desert is a wonderful place, and there's beauty in it. But it's also a great, wide space that provides good hiding places for some people."

"That's very true," Mrs. Arlington agreed. "Go ahead with your news, though—I'm curious, to say the least."

"Professor Anne, I received a phone call tonight from someone up in Visalia," Mrs. Edwards said, referring to a city about in the middle of the state. "A descendant of General Vallejo has heard a story passed down through the years, a story that came from one of General Sherman's men who worked with the Sutter group when gold was discovered at the saw mill."

"Interesting," Ashley noted. "So this person might know something about your saw blade?"

"Precisely," said Mrs. Edwards. "He said he needs to meet with me rather than go into anything over the phone or come to the press conference Monday—he sounds like a very private individual, which I respect. He doesn't want any media attention. I'm going to see him tomorrow. I don't care to drive that far, so I'm going to take the bus."

"All the way up there?" Mrs. Arlington asked.

"Yes, dear; it won't be a problem."

Mr. Arlington and Adam came back into the room from seeing Simon out. Mrs. Arlington asked Mrs. Edwards to hold a moment.

"Alex, Mrs. Edwards is on the phone," she told him. "We've filled her in on what happened here. She received a call from someone in Visalia, a descendant of a soldier who served under General Sherman. He wants to meet with her up there tomorrow. She's planning to take the bus . . ."

"Nonsense," Mr. Arlington replied. "Tell her we'll do the driving if she'd like. If we have time, we could drive to Sequoia National Park, too."

"Exactly what I was thinking," she smiled at him. She put the phone back up to her ear.

"Mrs. Edwards, we'd like to take you to Visalia tomorrow ourselves if that would be all right," she said. "We'd like to visit Sequoia National Park while we're up there."

There was a long pause.

"Why, that's very kind of you, but I couldn't impose on you and your family vacation like that. I'll be just fine."

"Mrs. Edwards, we really want to do this," Ashley interjected. "It will be fun. Adam and I are learning a lot about Sutter's Mill, and we'd like to learn more. And we're your friends now, so you're not imposing at all."

Mrs. Edwards chuckled. "Well, then, if you're sure, I'd be very grateful if you'd drive me," she said. "Can you be here early, say 7 A.M.?"

"Sure," Mrs. Arlington said.

"I'll make some flapjacks and sausage, so come hungry," Mrs. Edwards urged.

They hung up the phone, and Adam logged onto his laptop to print out driving directions to Visalia. After that, the family turned in for the evening, Ashley and Adam exhausted not only from their games, but from everything that had gone on since.

They had to be up early the next morning, and by the time they arrived at Mrs. Edwards's house, the teens were starving. When they got through with her home-cooked meal, there wasn't a flapjack or piece of sausage in sight.

"Before we get in the car, I have something special for you," Mrs. Edwards told the family. "It's a copy of General Sherman's own memoirs. I bought a few way back when because of the history of my family in this area during the Gold Rush and our involvement with Sutter's Mill. You kids have shown such an interest in history, I thought you might enjoy a copy."

Ashley and Adam accepted the book gratefully, but their mother held out her hands for it.

"It looks quite old and perhaps valuable," Mrs. Arlington said. "Are you sure you want to give this away?"

"Oh, Professor Anne, I have a couple more copies, and though it is an old printing, I still want you to have it. I bought extras, after all, to give out to my special friends, and you've certainly become that!"

Mrs. Arlington smiled and handed the book back to Adam, then everyone headed for the Arlingtons' SUV.

Once they were on their way, Adam asked if he could read from Sherman's memoirs aloud. Everyone was anxious to hear some of Sherman's story. Adam began with an excerpt describing Richard Barnes Mason, the newly arrived fifth military governor of California (1847–1849). The then-lieutenant Sherman would be working closely with the man and took the time to write down his impressions:

> Colonel R. B. Mason, First Dragoons, was an officer of great experience, deemed by some harsh and severe, but to me he seemed kind and agreeable. He had a large fund of good sense, and, during our long period of service together, I enjoyed his unlimited confidence.

"Do you know San Francisco's Fort Mason and Mason Street are named after him?" Mrs. Edwards asked the kids.

"At the time he was writing this, I believe he and Colonel Mason had offices in Monterey. But Sherman also had adventures around the state—I think he went to San Jose and also the quicksilver mines of New Almaden at different times."

"He was an adventurer, that's for sure," Adam said. He flipped to another section of the book. "Listen to this—here he mentions Sutter and his mill." Adam read:

> As the spring and summer of 1848 advanced, the reports came faster and faster from the gold mines at Sutter's sawmill. Stories reached us of fabulous discoveries, and spread throughout the land. Everybody was talking of "Gold! Gold!" until it assumed the character of a fever. Some of our soldiers began to desert; citizens were fitting out trains of wagons and pack mules to go to the mines. We heard of men earning fifty, five hundred, and thousands of dollars per day, and for a time it seemed somebody would reach solid gold. Some of this gold began to come to Yerba Buena San Francisco in trade, to disturb the value of merchandise, particularly of mules, horses, tin pans, and articles used in mining. I of course could not escape the infection, and at last convinced Colonel Mason that it was our duty to go up and see with our own eyes, that we might report the truth to our Government.

After reading some more and getting to know Mrs. Edwards a lot better, they arrived in Visalia shortly before noon. They soon found the address of the house they were looking for. Vance Vallejo and his wife, Teresa, a middle-aged couple, welcomed Mrs. Edwards and the Arlingtons into their home, a nice, two-story residence with an immaculately manicured front lawn.

"Mrs. Edwards, it's a pleasure," Mr. Vallejo said, helping her through the door and into the living room. The purring of the air conditioner and the soft sounds of music greeted the guests. While it was very warm outside, the house was nice and cool. Mrs. Vallejo passed around a tray of sandwiches and soft drinks.

After a few minutes of getting to know one another, Mrs. Edwards showed the Vallejos her piece of the letter from her ancestor Arnold Atkinson.

"Atkinson, Atkinson, that name rings a bell," Mr. Vallejo said. "I have the main items out here that I need to show you, but I may have some sort of documentation that mentions an Atkinson, too. Please excuse me while I find it."

He brought out a folder full of papers, most of them obviously very old and faded.

"In the end of June, 1848, with the Gold Rush mentality at a fevered pace, General Sherman planned a trip to the just uncovered gold mines at Sutter's Fort," Mr. Vallejo explained. "He crossed the Bay and went to San Rafael before visiting my great-great-grandfather, General Vallejo, at Sonoma. Next he headed to New Helvitia and then to Sutter's Fort. It was there he met this man, A. Atkinson."

"Wow!" Adam said. "It's probably Arnold Atkinson."

Mrs. Edwards was also excited by this news, so Mr. Vallejo continued. "Here's the interesting part, and this is something that finally makes sense—though it didn't completely until you mentioned Arnold Atkinson," he said. "You see, I had no idea how it linked to you, Mrs. Edwards, except for the sawmill relic theft that we heard about on the radio. Now, though, the Atkinson name provides another piece to the puzzle from our end of it."

Mrs. Edwards nodded appreciatively.

"A soldier from Sutter's Mill had gone to join General Vallejo's troops at Sonoma, and he told a story about this man at the mill, A. Atkinson," Mr. Vallejo explained. "They were running a piece of wood through the sawmill, when suddenly the saw blade came to a very quick, noisy halt. What Sutter wanted was lumber to sell to the settlers—he wasn't particularly thrilled about gold because he thought it would be a nuisance and bring in more nuisances to get in the way of his sawmill operations. He may have been lacking in lumber, but at least he wasn't lacking in machinery parts. They took out the piece of wood that damaged the blade and put in a new blade."

The story wasn't completely new to the Arlingtons or Mrs. Edwards, who had perhaps owned that very damaged blade—except now that it was stolen she couldn't be sure.

Mr. Vallejo reached into the bag he was holding and pulled out a piece of wood a foot long and three inches wide.

"This was given to General Vallejo, and he showed it to General Sherman at their meeting," Mr. Vallejo said. "This is the piece of wood that stopped the sawmill. There's a big chunk out of it here where perhaps an embedded rock or something caused the machine to jam."

Ashley deduced the significance of the piece of lumber. "So not only was this piece of wood part of Gold Rush history and put through Sutter's Mill by Arnold Atkinson," she mused, "but it was also held in the hands of General Vallejo and General Sherman. That's amazing!"

"This is rightfully yours, then," Mr. Vallejo said to Mrs. Edwards, handing her the wood. "We believe this is the very piece of wood 'A. Atkinson' was using. It never dawned on me till meeting you today, but obviously your ancestor Atkinson gave this piece to the man who left to go to Sonoma. That man passed it along to General Vallejo.

So this went from your relative through a middle man, so to speak, to my relative."

Ashley went over and sat next to Mrs. Edwards, putting her arm around the older woman. "So now the circle is complete," she said as Mrs. Edwards wiped away a tear.

Mrs. Edwards ran her hands along the wood and wondered aloud at how her hands were tracing the same path that Atkinson, General Vallejo, and General Sherman had traced more than a century and a half earlier.

"If we can just find the blade, then the circle will be unbroken," said Adam.

"That's such a shame to have it stolen like that," Mr. Vallejo said, shaking his head. "But you realize that if we had not heard about the theft over the radio, we would never have heard of you and been able to make this incredible connection. Certainly I'm not implying that the theft was in any way a good thing. However, at least we were able to find a silver lining in it. Though I should apologize for making you drive all the way up here."

"It was well worth the trip," Mrs. Arlington said.

Mrs. Edwards agreed it had been quite worthwhile. "I'd have walked this far for this," she said jokingly. "I've learned some important details about my family history and made some great new friends."

"This wood is a relic all by itself," Adam commented. "But don't you wonder why a little piece of rock embedded in it would be such a big deal, enough to shut down the mill operations? We're still not sure why the sawmill blade stopped working when this piece was fed through it. It doesn't seem like a rock would be that big of a deal."

Ashley suddenly stood as an important possibility hit her. "Gold?" she asked.

Treasure or Trouble?

Everyone looked at Ashley. Clearly, she had their undivided attention.

"My guess is that it was a gold nugget," Ashley said.

Everyone's eyes opened wide. Yes, indeed, gold would have made the whole episode a significant event at the sawmill, much more so than if an embedded rock or a knot in the wood had stopped the saw blade.

"I think, somehow a piece of gold became lodged within this piece of lumber—or maybe the wooden log it came from was found in a stream that had a lot of gold in it," she said. "Maybe there was a hole or deformity in the log to begin with, and the gold nugget became stuck in it and hidden somehow from sight. Then the log was taken to the sawmill and run through, and poof, the blade hit the gold!"

Mr. and Mrs. Arlington, along with everyone else, were impressed. The theory, while it would take a while to pan out, was certainly more than possible, even plausible.

"Would the gold still be in the blade?" Adam asked.

Ashley shrugged her shoulders. "That's a good question. My guess would be that it's probably not. However, I'd also guess that the gold left a noticeable mark in the blade—and that's the basis for the story being passed down through generations. There's a great story behind all this—that much we know for certain. But does it lead to anything more than the damaged saw blade? I don't know."

Mrs. Arlington rose and straightened the pillow on the couch. "We should be on our way. We'd like to spend a few hours at Sequoia National Park this afternoon. We'll give Detective Simon a call tonight," she said. "This is some good information. We don't want to do anything to impede the investigation, of course, and I don't know if this provides the thieves with a motive or if it's just relevant information. But it could give a context as far as what they're looking for and why. Certainly, the gold angle adds a whole new dimension to the case."

The Arlingtons and Mrs. Edwards thanked the Vallejos for their hospitality and insights, as well as the incredible piece of history they had given to Mrs. Edwards.

"Keep us posted," Mrs. Vallejo said to them on their way out. "We'd love to hear how this turns out. We'll keep you in our thoughts and hope for a happy ending!"

It was far too soon to know if there would be a happy ending, but it could lean that way if only the police in Palmdale had caught the thieves and recovered the blade by the time the car full of history hunters returned to town.

The drive to the national park went quickly as Adam read some more from General Sherman's memoirs, relating how Sherman's party crossed the Bay.

"Here's the part that tells about what the Vallejos gave us today," Adam told the others. "It talks about him meeting General Vallejo at Sonoma. It picks up where they arrived at Sutter's Fort." He read aloud:

At that time there was not the sign of a habitation there or thereabouts, except at the fort, and an old adobe-house, east of the fort, known as the hospital. The fort itself was one of adobe-walls, about twenty feet high, rectangular in form, with two-story block houses at diagonal corners. The entrance was by a large gate, open by day and closed at night, with two iron ship's guns near at hand. Inside there was a large house, with a good shingle-roof, used as a storehouse, and all around the walls were ranged rooms, the fort-wall being the outer wall of the house. The inner wall was also of adobe. These rooms were used by Captain Sutter and by his people. He had a blacksmith's shop, a carpenter's shop, and other rooms where women made blankets.

Sutter was monarch of all he surveyed and had authority to inflict punishment even unto death, a power he did not fail to use. He had horses, cattle, and sheep, and of these he gave generously to all in need. He ordered driven into our camp cattle and some sheep, which were slaughtered for our use. Already the gold mines were beginning to be felt. Many people were then encamped, some going and some coming, all full of gold stories, and each surpassing the other.

"It's like history coming to life," Ashley said.

"You feel like you are right there," Mrs. Edwards nodded in agreement. "Oh, my, just look at that spectacular view," she observed, looking out the car window.

"Wish we had more time to enjoy this park," said Mr. Arlington, pulling into a parking space at an overlook.

"Yeah, we should at least try to find the largest sequoia in the park," said Adam. "I read on a web site that it's called the General Sherman Tree!"

Everyone laughed, but they did find the tree and thoroughly enjoyed the beauty of the park.

After the family stopped for supper, Adam finished the trip back to Palmdale by reading Sherman's account of finally reaching the sawmill Sutter had constructed:

Labor in the form of good workers was scarce and expensive, so the mill was built to save labor. After arranging his headrace, dam, and tub-wheel, he let on water to test the goodness of his machinery. It worked very well until it was found that the tailrace did not carry off water fast enough, so he put his men to work to clear out the tailrace. They scratched a ditch down the middle of the dry channel over which the mill was built, throwing the coarser stones to one side. Then, letting on the water again, it would run with speed down this channel, washing away the dirt, saving the workers labor. This was repeated several times, and as the foreman, Marshall, was working the ditch, he observed particles of yellow metal which he gathered up in his hand; it suddenly flashed across his mind that they were gold.

After picking up about an ounce, he hurried down to the fort to report to Captain Sutter his discovery. Captain Sutter himself related to me Marshall's account, saying that as he sat in his room at the fort one day in February or March of 1848, a knock was heard at the door. He called out, "Come in," and it was his foreman, Marshall. That day he looked strangely wild, and Sutter asked him what was the matter. Marshall then asked the captain if anyone was within hearing, and peered about the room and even under the bed.

"What is it, man?" Sutter demanded of him. "Has there been an accident at the mill?" Sutter even began making his way to the door, fearful a terrible calamity had taken place. At last Marshall revealed the pellicles of gold from the ditch, laying them before the captain. Sutter attached less importance to the discovery than Marshall, and told him to go back to the mill and say nothing of what he had seen.

Mrs. Edwards interrupted, "It's understandable why Sutter wasn't passionately excited by the discovery of the gold. His passion was his sawmill, not panning for the gold nuggets in its tailrace."

Adam finished reading them the account:

Yet Sutter, knowing the discovery might add value to the sawmill location, dispatched men to our headquarters at Monterey. They asked for a preemption to the quarter-section of land at Coloma, which we were not in authority to grant them, as I previously related.

For his part, Marshall obeyed and returned to the mill, but by some means the other workers learned his secret. They wanted to gather in the gold, but Marshall threatened to shoot them if they attempted it. The other men employed, however, had sense enough to know that if 'placer' gold existed at Coloma, it would also be found farther downstream, so they gradually 'prospected' until they reached Mormon Island fifteen miles below the mill, where they discovered one of the richest placers on earth. They also let out the secret to other of Sutter's employees, Mormons working at his gristmill six miles above the fort on the American Fork of the river. All of them struck for high wages, to which Sutter had to yield to keep them, until they asked for ten dollars a day. He refused, and the two mills on which he had spent so much money were never completed and fell into decay.

"The Gold Rush wasn't much of a boon for Sutter as far as his mill projects were concerned, was it?" Mrs. Arlington commented. "What's treasure to some is trouble to others."

Mr. Arlington pulled the car into Mrs. Edwards's driveway at almost 10 P.M., and the group decided to call Detective Simon from her house. Simon, however, had little news for them.

"A couple of wild goose chases today, that's all," he told Mr. Arlington. "We never realized how many green pickups there are in this county until now. It's almost like trying to find a needle in a haystack, even with the county police helicopter we had in the air for a good six hours. Of course, if those guys are moving at night, it will be that much harder to track them. We're not giving up hope by any means, though."

Mr. Arlington told Simon about the piece of wood the Vallejos gave Mrs. Edwards, the very piece that had apparently caused the sawmill blade to cease functioning so long ago.

"Please tell her I'll be out in the morning to take a look at it," Simon said. "Of course it now belongs to her, and there's no reason for us to take it in as evidence, but it could fill in some gaps for us."

Mr. Arlington hung up, and the family headed back to their hotel suite, where Mrs. Arlington took care of returning some of her phone calls while Mr. Arlington handled his correspondence via e-mail.

"I'm too wound up to sleep," Ashley said to Adam. "Let's head to the weight room."

The teens spotted each other during some lifting exercises, then ran side-by-side on a pair of treadmills.

"I can't believe you picked up on that gold nugget angle," Adam said to his sister. "That was pretty bright—it seems really probable now that I think about it."

Ashley brushed at some sweat with her towel. "It just seems to make sense," she said. "Any antique is a special thing, but to have thieves come out to an elderly woman's house for an antique blade? Highly unlikely. That kind of thing can probably be found across the Midwest and all over. There had to be something special about this particular blade that gives it more value—something completely unique. What's your theory?"

Adam slowed his treadmill to catch his breath. "I thought it had something to do with history. Maybe it was made in a special place where only a few others were made. But I like your theory better—what if there is some gold dust or something left on the blade?"

Ashley's eyes lit up. "That would explain why some people want to get their hands on it!" she cried.

Just then Mr. and Mrs. Arlington walked in together.

"Time to call it a night," Mrs. Arlington said to the kids. "And we have some other news that you might not enjoy too much. We're leaving in the morning for Barstow. Your father's business meeting was moved up a day, and I can take care of some business there as well. We're not leaving you kids behind, and we'll have a good time."

"But Mom, Dad," Ashley pleaded, "we can't just take off now! Tomorrow's Monday, and even though there's no saw blade left to see, the big brainstorming meeting about who took it and why is still at Mrs. Edwards's house. We were going to be there. . . ."

"Yeah, and what about Ash's theory about the gold nugget stopping the blade in the first place? That could be an important idea to share if it provides a motive for the crime," Adam added.

"Guys, we can fill Detective Simon in on that idea over the phone," Mr. Arlington said. "Gold or no gold, we have to hit the road."

Burglar Business in Barstow

Adam and Ashley headed up to the suite with their parents. After showers, they sat on their parents' bed for a talk.

"Listen, you two, we'll pick this up when we get back—first thing," Mrs. Arlington told them, running her hand through Ashley's hair. "And we'll even check in with both Mrs. Edwards and Detective Simon while we're on the road, okay?"

The teens knew there was no point in trying to negotiate a longer stay. They'd get back this way as soon as they could; meanwhile, their parents had business in Barstow. They went downstairs and logged on to Adam's laptop. They went online to find out more about John Sutter, and Ashley located a copy of an article from *Hutchings' California Magazine* dated November 1857. It was titled "The

Discovery of Gold in California," and the author was none other than General John A. Sutter himself. He wrote:

So soon as the secret of gold discovery was out my laborers began to leave me, in small parties first, but then all left, from the clerk to the cook, and I was in great distress; only a few mechanics remained to finish some very necessary work . . . and about eight invalids, who continued slowly to work a few teams.

The Mormons did not like to leave my mill unfinished, but they got the gold fever like everybody else. So long as these people have been employed by me they have behaved very well, and were industrious and faithful laborers. . . .

Then the people commenced rushing up from San Francisco and other parts of California; in May 1848: in the former village only five men were left to take care of the women and children. The single men locked their doors and left for "Sutter's Fort," and from there to Eldorado. For some time the people in Monterey and farther south would not believe the news of the gold discovery, and said that it was only a "Ruse de Guerre" of Sutter's, because he wanted to have neighbors in his wilderness. From this time on I got only too many neighbors, and some very bad ones among them. What a great misfortune was this sudden gold discovery for me! It had just broken up and ruined my hard, restless, and industrious labors, connected with many dangers of life, as I had many narrow escapes before I became properly established. From my mill buildings I reaped no benefit whatever, the mill stones even have been stolen and sold. . . .

By this sudden discovery of gold, all my great plans were destroyed. Had I succeeded for a few years before the gold was discovered, I would have been the richest citizen on the Pacific shore; but it had to be different. Instead of being rich, I am ruined. . . .

Adam glanced at Ashley.

"Unbelievable," Ashley said to her brother. "One man's riches were another man's undoing, in a way."

The kids decided to call it a night, disconnecting the computer from the phone and shutting it down. Adam carefully packed it in its case for the trip the following day, hoping they would get a chance to use it while their parents were busy.

When they were ready to leave the next morning, Mrs. Arlington asked the kids what they wanted to do while she and their father took care of business in Barstow.

"Could we maybe tour the local newspaper?" Adam asked. "I have the number for the *Barstow Desert Dispatch*. We could learn a little about the town and see how they put out their paper. It's a small daily, and since Ash and I have been to the *Washington Post* several times, it might be kind of cool to see how a smaller community newspaper does its job."

"Great idea," Mr. Arlington said, so Adam called the *Desert Dispatch* to make the arrangements.

The managing editor, Tim Merrill, said that would be fine if Adam and Ashley stopped by to meet with him. He would give them "the full nickel tour."

"If it's all right with your parents, I could take you down to lunch at Barstow Station, too," Merrill said. "It's just down the street from the paper; my lunch schedule is open, no interviews till later today, and we can walk."

Adam got permission from his parents and relayed that to Mr. Merrill, then thanked him and said they would be there a little before noon.

The drive to Barstow was shorter than the Arlingtons expected, though it was on a roller-coaster, up-and-down state highway to Victorville, where they picked up Interstate 15 north to Barstow.

As Mr. Arlington pulled up to the stop sign at their Barstow exit off-ramp, he looked both ways to make sure he could turn. Out of the corner of his eye he noticed something odd under the nearby bridge.

"That . . . that truck over there," he said, pointing to the left, under the overpass. "Could that be—? No way! Hold on, I'm taking a left here."

"Why? We're supposed to go right—what are you seeing?" his wife questioned him.

Adam and Ashley were straining to see out the window on the driver's side.

"That's the truck," Ashley suddenly proclaimed. "That's the one the thieves had in the parking lot of our hotel!"

Adam saw the top of the orange tarp as they pulled closer, but there was nothing under it in the bed of the truck.

"Stop, Dad! We need to check it out," he said.

"No way," his dad firmly replied. "I will slow down, though, and we'll try for a closer look, but act as inconspicuously as possible. If those two guys are in the front, they could get jumpy if they notice us all staring at them."

Clearly, there was no one inside the truck when the Arlingtons drove by. Mr. Arlington turned the SUV around about a block past the bridge, and they went by the truck again.

Ashley opened her backpack and took out a notebook. She copied down the truck's license plate number.

"Cell phone, please," Mrs. Arlington said to her husband. "I'm going to call Detective Simon." She took the phone and retrieved Simon's number from her purse.

"I'll pull into this station here and fill up with gas. We're low anyway," Mr. Arlington decided. "You kids keep an eye on that truck and see if anyone comes around it while your mother makes the call."

"Detective Simon," Mrs. Arlington said into the phone as her husband got out of the car, "this is Anne Arlington. We've driven to Barstow on business. Alex's meeting got moved up a day; that's why we can't attend your meeting at Mrs. Edwards's today. I think we can still help with the investigation, though—as we pulled off the exit here, we spotted the green pickup truck under the overpass."

"In Barstow—the green truck is in Barstow?" he repeated, making sure he had heard correctly.

"Yes, we're sure it's the same truck we saw, with the same tarp in the back." She motioned toward Ashley to hand her the notebook. "Ashley wrote down the license plate number," she told Simon, relaying the number to him.

"Good work, you all should have badges," Simon said. "I'll have the local authorities out there in a few minutes."

"Do you want us to stay here till they come?" Mrs. Arlington asked him.

"Are the thieves anywhere in sight?" Simon queried.

"It doesn't appear so," she said.

"Then if you're a comfortable distance away and can keep an eye on that truck till the officers get there, that would be great. I can have a cruiser there in less than five minutes. But I'd recommend you stay as far away from it as you can."

"We'll do that," Mrs. Arlington assured him. "We'll call you back this afternoon."

"Sounds good," Simon said, then he hung up to call in the sighting.

Adam and Ashley kept an eye on the truck as their dad filled up their SUV with gas. Even before he finished paying for it, a police car was on the scene. The teens immediately wanted to go talk to the policemen and see if there were any clues inside the truck.

"We'd be very out of line doing that," Mr. Arlington told them. "Detective Simon will be in contact with the authorities here, and we'll head on our way and find out later if anything comes out of this."

Mr. Arlington drove to the attorney's office where his meeting was scheduled, and Mrs. Arlington scooted into the driver's seat. She went to the newspaper office and met Tim Merrill.

"Thanks for making time for our kids," she said as she and the kids shook Merrill's hand. "They actually heard about your paper when they were studying the 'Erin Brockovich' story in school. One of the programs on television mentioned your newspaper."

Merrill smiled. He knew that the events that had transpired in Hinckley, which was within the *Desert Dispatch*'s readership area, had gained the town and his newspaper some notoriety.

"I think your kids will have a good time today," Merrill told Mrs. Arlington. "And it's always good to see teens who want to make the most out of a visit and learn about the locality—that's a rare thing!"

"I'll be back for you about 2:00," she told Ashley and Adam. "If Mr. Merrill needs to get back to work before then, you two can explore a little bit, but stay close to the newspaper office. I'll pick you up in front in about two hours."

Ashley and Adam said they'd be there to meet her on time, and she headed to Barstow Community College, where she had to get some material from one of the professors for a class she was teaching back home in D.C.

Mrs. Arlington picked up her material, then decided to stop at a campus information desk to pick up a catalog so she could compare the courses to what she was teaching back home. She often did that when they stopped at colleges and universities across the nation.

The young woman who was seated behind the sliding glass window at the desk was very helpful. Mrs. Arlington felt someone behind her and stepped to the side so the man could be seen by the information girl. She moved aside to be polite, but she didn't really look at the man's face. After receiving the catalog of courses, however, she turned to the side and said, "Excuse me," to the man, who was obviously in a hurry. He nearly bumped into her, stepping forward to the window as soon as she moved aside.

"Oh, sorry," he apologized, taking a step to avoid a collision.

Mrs. Arlington finally looked directly at him, also trying to avoid a collision.

It's him! she thought to herself. *One of the thieves!*

Near-Collision
with a Criminal

Trying to keep the man from noticing her surprise, Mrs. Arlington backed up a few steps and opened the catalog, pretending to be looking through it to find a class. She couldn't call the police right there in front of him, so she decided to get a little closer and take a good look at the short, stocky man. Cleverly, she came up with a question for the girl at the desk.

"Excuse me, this is the fall guide of classes—is the spring one out now, or anytime soon?" she asked her.

"No, I'm sorry, the spring semester catalogs don't come out until at least midway through the fall semester," the girl told Mrs. Arlington.

Since the man was watching the girl's response, Mrs. Arlington took a moment to get a good look at his features—a pair of bushy eyebrows, a balding spot in the back of his head, and sideburns that reached the bottom of his earlobes. His eyes were so dark brown that they appeared black, and he had at least two or three days' growth of facial hair.

"Well, all right then, thank you," Mrs. Arlington told the girl, backing away.

The man, slightly annoyed, looked at Mrs. Arlington. Then he asked the girl his own question.

"Who would someone go to at this college if they wanted to know something about lumber machines and maybe about metals—maybe even precious metals?" he inquired.

Mrs. Arlington almost jumped out of her shoes. If there had been any doubt before, his question confirmed his identity.

Surely, she thought to herself, *he's trying to find a professor who can tell him and his accomplice just what it is they've stolen. They must not realize the value of it, and they want to find out fast.*

On the one hand it was a brazen move, strolling into a college office and asking to see a professor who might help them out unwittingly. On the other hand, the thieves were probably thinking they couldn't very well ask a professor back at Antelope Valley, too close to the scene of their crime.

Mrs. Arlington reached into her purse and grabbed Simon's card. She felt for the cell phone as she moved away casually and realized she had left it with her husband. She spotted a pay phone just outside the doors of the building, and through the glass window she could keep an eye on the thief while she made a call.

As the wind helped blow the door open, she hurried out to the phone. She quickly dialed Simon's number, though the process took a good minute or so because she had to use her phone card to place the long-distance call. It seemed like Simon would never answer, but on the fourth ring he picked it up.

"It's Anne Arlington, and I just saw one of the thieves," she said excitedly, but in an intentionally subdued voice.

"Where are you, Anne?" Simon asked.

"At Barstow Community College outside the main administration building," she said. "He's asking for a professor who knows about lumbering equipment and metals—it's him, I just know it's him!"

"Hang on and I'll go to my office phone here and call the Barstow police," Simon said. "I'll be back."

As he put her on hold, Mrs. Arlington turned and looked back through the glass. The hallway in front of the administration desk was empty.

Oh no! she thought. *He's gone!*

Just then the door came flying open and the man came out. He quickly hurried down the steps, not even noticing her.

The man hurried to a van on the other side of the parking lot. Mrs. Arlington set the pay phone receiver down. She wanted to get a good look at what kind of van the man had gotten into. She suspected he and his accomplice had deserted the green truck the family had seen under the bridge.

The van was too far away for her to get a license plate number. In fact, the sun was so bright that it was hard to even determine the exact color of the van. Mrs. Arlington didn't want to cover her eyes, using her hands as a visor, because the driver—the other man they had seen in the hotel parking lot—was looking her way and might become suspicious.

They'll have to come this way, she thought to herself. *It's a one-way drive—they'll pass right in front of me on their way out. I'll get the license plate number and a better description then!*

Her hopes were quickly dashed when the driver threw the van in reverse, backed up about forty feet the wrong way on the one-way, and went out the entrance, just beating an SUV pulling into the lot. She picked up the receiver again and heard Simon's voice. She could also hear sirens in the distance, meaning the police must be on the way to the college.

"Anne! Are you there, Anne? Are you all right? Is anyone there?" Simon was saying on the other end of the line.

"I'm here," she assured Simon. "I wasn't close enough to get a license number, but I can describe the van the two men left in. It's a minivan, dark in color, maybe maroon or dark brown—the sun was in my eyes. It's got a luggage rack on top and looks like an older model. Looks like they're headed out to the interstate."

"Okay, I'll call the Barstow police back with your information—don't even think of pursuing those men! That would be far too dangerous, and unlawful."

Unlike her children, Mrs. Arlington didn't need to be sold on that point. "I can guarantee you my part of this chase ended at the sidewalk," she told Simon.

"Good job," he replied. "At least this way, we can prevent them from getting out of state. The interstate breaks off toward Arizona one way and toward Las Vegas the other. I'll have both routes blocked within a few minutes of now. If nothing else, we know what they've switched to driving. I'm going to go now. Thanks!"

"Okay. The police are here and the thieves aren't, so I'll go talk to the officers. Good-bye."

She hung up and stepped out of the phone booth. She met the police officers and introduced herself, giving them her information as they walked to the girl at the information desk. The officers asked the girl to restate the conversation she had had with the thief and describe any other details she might have noted about him, then they thanked her and Mrs. Arlington for their time. On the way outside, they told Mrs. Arlington they would be in contact with Detective Simon the rest of the day, so she could find out about anything they uncovered through him.

Mrs. Arlington was shaken up a bit by being so close to one of the suspects. She decided to try to calm down, purchasing some bottled water from a vending machine and sitting down for a moment. She hoped the thieves could be caught before long, and perhaps the saw blade was in the minivan and could be recovered without further incident. Looking at her watch, she saw it was almost 2 P.M. She walked to her SUV and headed toward the newspaper office to pick up Ashley and Adam.

Back at the newspaper, Merrill had started the tour by taking Ashley and Adam around the offices. The entire news, circulation, and advertising departments were all located on the same floor of the building, with no walls separating the various areas. That was in stark contrast to the *Washington Post,* which was several stories high.

"But that's just one of the big differences between one of the country's major dailies and what we practice here, which we call community journalism," Merrill said. "We don't cover the globe here—our wire services handle that. We just cover our corner of the world here in the high desert."

After Mr. Merrill answered all their questions and introduced them to some of the staff, he walked them down to Barstow Station. It was built on a train station theme, with several "box cars" to eat in at the fast food restaurants located there. Over lunch, the teens filled Merrill in on what they had stumbled onto with the sawmill blade and its theft.

"I heard that report on the radio," Merrill said. "We ran a brief on that. You two kids would make terrific reporters, the way you ask questions and find things out. I wanted to know more about that story myself."

"Well, then, you're going to like this next one," Adam said. "The green pickup truck we told you about—the one used in the theft of the sawmill blade—has been found under the overpass south of town."

"Here?" Merrill exclaimed. "I'll have one of my reporters call about that! The police here are pretty good about contact with us, and it's one of our reporter's jobs to check in with them each afternoon. I'm sure the police will be preparing a press release, and we'll follow up on it to make sure we get all the facts in the paper tomorrow. If they haven't caught the thieves yet, maybe we can get descriptions of the guys and the public can help the police out."

Adam and Ashley decided not to give him their own descriptions. "We better act as bystanders, not news sources in this," Ashley explained to Merrill. "Mom, Dad, and Detective Simon would prefer it that way."

"I understand," Merrill assured them. "I don't want to put you two kids on the spot, and we won't mention you in the story. But thanks for the news tip!"

When they got back to the *Desert Dispatch,* Merrill showed them the archives where the back issues of the newspaper were stored and invited them to peruse the papers while they waited for their mom to pick them up.

"Thanks for your time and for lunch," Ashley told Merrill as she and Adam shook his hand. "It was nice of you to make time for us."

"Any time," Merrill smiled. He reached into his wallet. "Here's my card. If you ever need anything else, feel free to call or e-mail me."

"Thanks!" Adam said. He and Ashley then went and read through some of the local papers till their mother pulled up at 2:15.

Meeting her outside, they filled her in on the events of their afternoon.

"Barstow Station was terrific, but the newspaper was even better," Ashley told her mom. "You should see how detailed they are about covering local things like school sports and board meetings. It's pretty neat for the people in the community."

"Pretty enlightening stuff," their mom commented. "That's one difference between a major metropolis and a smaller city or rural area—more personalized services and news coverage. By the way, I had a pretty exciting afternoon myself," she told them.

"How's that, Mom?" Adam asked. "Did you meet some of the college's history professors when you picked up the catalog?"

"Not exactly, but when I picked up my catalog I met someone else."

"Who?" both teens asked curiously.

"I believe he was, well, one of the suspects . . ." Mrs. Arlington said.

Adam and Ashley gasped.

"What? You met him? No way!" Adam cried. Then, "Are you all right? Tell us what happened—is he in custody?"

"Not exactly," Mrs. Arlington said, "though I hope the police have caught up with him and his cohort by now." She recounted the events for the kids and told them the thieves were now driving what was probably a stolen minivan.

"Did you call Detective Simon and the police?" Ashley asked.

"Of course I did," her mom responded.

Adam nudged Ashley. "We should have gone with Mom," he said. "We had fun, but it was nothing like what Mom experienced. I would have traded our burgers in a boxcar for seeing one of the suspects!"

Mrs. Arlington smiled. "It's probably better that you weren't with me, since you're such a cowboy about this sort of thing, tough guy," she told Adam. "I did all I could to see what kind of car they were driving and where they were headed, and Detective Simon warned me that I had gone far enough. I can just see you on the scene—you'd have been wanting to go look into their car windows for the sawmill blade or chase them down the road as they left!"

"Probably," Adam said with a grin. He and his sister were really wound up now, developing theories left and right about what the suspects were thinking, how they escaped from Lancaster to the high desert, and how they abandoned the pickup and attained another vehicle.

"They probably wanted a car they could store the sawmill blade inside," Adam guessed. "With that tarp on the back of the pickup, it was a neon light—an orange one. They probably felt like sitting ducks!"

"I think I can guess how they made it from Lancaster to Barstow undetected," Ashley mused. "They probably went the back highways and even the dirt roads, and I'd also guess that they know the whole area fairly well—at least one of them does, anyway—and they know how to use the country back roads to avoid the police."

Mrs. Arlington told the two kids that it would be a good time to check in with Detective Simon again and also put in a call to Mrs. Edwards. There was no answer when Adam dialed Mrs. Edwards's number, and she had no answering machine or voice mail. Ashley, however, got through to Detective Simon.

"Hello, it's Ashley Arlington checking in to see if you have any further updates for us," she told him.

"Actually, Ashley, is your mother right there? . . . Good. Several things have happened in the last couple of hours since she saw the suspect at the college. It's a good news, bad news kind of thing. Tell her the fingerprints taken off the pickup truck you guys spotted gave us the names of the two thieves who stole the blade—actually, the truck also was stolen, as it turns out. The thieves, including the one your mom almost literally ran into at the college, are a couple of twice-convicted felons both recently out on parole. Both have convictions of burglary and theft, so this crime is sort of par for the course for them. Though neither has ever shot anyone, we're going on the assumption that they are armed and dangerous, because we have no reason to believe anything else. Should you run into them again, and I know that's a long shot, continue to be very, very careful. So if—make that *when*—we capture them, they'll be doing life in prison without parole because of our state's 'three-strike' law, which sends three-time convicted felons to prison for life. That looks promising. The convicts do have some friends in the area just outside of Barstow, and we're running down those leads right now."

Ashley took a minute to relay what Simon had told her to her mom and Adam, then she told Simon how pleased her mom was about the positive identification due to the fingerprints.

"We haven't gotten to the bad news yet," Simon reminded Ashley. Then he paused. "I don't think I better tell you this over the phone," he said. "I don't want to rattle you kids. Maybe I should talk to your mom instead."

"I can respect that, Detective Simon, if that's your choice. She's right here. But I'd really like to know—we can handle it," Ashley said to him. "I'm sure we can. Mom would probably tell us anyway."

Simon paused another moment. "Okay, Ashley," he agreed. "You and your brother are very mature for your ages, and you've been a big help on this case. I can talk to your mother afterwards. Now, I don't want to alarm you," he said slowly, "but Mrs. Edwards might be missing."

Chapter 11

Peril in Palmdale?

Ashley nearly dropped the phone. Her jaw dropped wide open, and both her mother and Adam sensed that something was wrong.

"What's going on?" Adam demanded.

Ashley gathered her composure and told them, "Mrs. Edwards *might* be missing, but the police are still unsure at this point."

She put the phone back up to her ear. "I told Mom and Adam," she said to Simon. "There's nothing definite, though, right? I mean, there could be an explanation?"

"That's surely what we're hoping," Simon said. "We haven't been able to track her down this afternoon. We had a short brainstorming meeting at her house this morning, and I had to go back a few hours later to check something at the crime scene. She was gone. The good news is that there were no signs of foul play at her house. The doors were locked, and when we went in, we didn't see anything amiss. However, she is a very special elderly person, and it certainly isn't like her to be gone. We haven't classified her as a missing person—yet—but we do want to find her as soon as possible. I'm concerned about her, but until some more time passes, I don't want to come across as being alarmed."

The three Arlingtons were already alarmed.

"Wait till Dad hears this!" Adam said to his mom.

"We should be back to the hotel in a couple of hours," Ashley was finishing with Detective Simon. "You can reach us there if you need to."

"Have a safe drive back," he told Ashley, "and thank your mom for me for her role today. She thought quickly on her feet, and seeing how these guys are considered armed and dangerous, we're glad she used good judgment and exercised caution. I'll talk to you again soon. Good-bye."

Mrs. Arlington and the kids went by the attorney's office to pick up Mr. Arlington. He was already waiting and saw them from a window as they pulled up.

"Did you all have an interesting day while I was in my meeting?" he asked as he slid into the driver's seat of their SUV.

Mrs. Arlington and the kids smiled.

"Not really," Ashley said.

"Not really?" he asked.

"Not unless you count Mom almost running into one of the suspects at the college. He was trying to find a professor who knew about antique sawmills and gold," Ashley said, smiling.

"You're kidding me!" her dad said.

"No, we're not, actually," his wife told him. "I really did sight one of the suspects at the college—he nearly bumped into me, and from a phone booth outside I called Detective Simon and watched as the thief and his accomplice got into their current vehicle, a minivan, and drove away."

"Did they suspect you were observing them?" Mr. Arlington asked her in alarm.

"Of course not," she said. "Like I told Detective Simon on the phone, my chase ended at the sidewalk. I wasn't about to get mixed up with that man, but I was able to get some good descriptive information and a license plate number for the police."

"I know you can take care of yourself, but I still wish I had been with you!" Mr. Arlington said.

"Two of us might really have looked suspicious making that call from the phone booth, dear," she told him with a laugh. "But there is more you should know. When we checked in with Detective Simon later he told us Mrs. Edwards might—only *might*—be missing. She's not at home, nor is there any sign of where she is. But there's no sign of foul play either."

"That's not good at all!" Mr. Arlington exclaimed. "Now I wish I'd been with her today, too. If I had been aware of all this earlier, I'd never have kept my mind on my meeting—I'd never have stayed!"

"We'll definitely have to check with Detective Simon for an update tonight," Ashley said to her father.

"Absolutely," he said, "but what about your day? How was the newspaper office?"

Ashley told her dad all about the *Barstow Desert Dispatch* and their time with Tim Merrill. Then, in the middle of Adam's description of Barstow Station and its restaurants, the family passed a sheriff's flatbed tow truck. It was towing the thieves' green pickup. Suddenly the saw blade theft completely occupied their thoughts again.

"Look at that!" Mr. Arlington exclaimed. "I'll bet it's headed back to Lancaster to Simon and his coworkers who are on the case. They probably want to comb through it again."

"Makes you wonder where the thieves and the saw blade are now," Ashley said. "At least the police have a description of the 'new' getaway car, though, thanks to Mom!"

"I don't think those two had any idea what they were stealing. I mean, how could they?" Adam said. "If they had a plan, they would have known what to do with the blade, like take it to an overseas antique dealer or something. I'm thinking they just heard the report of the relic on the radio and wanted to cash in, with no real idea of exactly what they were getting—or exactly what to do with it."

"My feeling is they thought they could possibly get rid of it in Las Vegas," said Ashley as she looked at the atlas. "If that failed, then they could have headed to a pawn shop and just sold it for whatever they could get."

Both theories seemed to make sense.

"That criminal mentality just breeds itself," Mrs. Arlington observed.

"That's true! I see it all the time in court," her husband put in. "Think about it: These two guys finally get out of prison for what sounds like at least the second time, and they go right back to crime, knowing that if they get caught, they'll never get out again. And since they've been arrested and prosecuted at least twice before, you'd think they'd have a good hunch they'd be busted again. Yet they went back to a life of crime anyway, even with that 'three-strikes' law hanging over their heads. That's not much of a life."

Mr. Arlington took the highway exit for Palmdale, and after having pizza at a nearby restaurant, they pulled into the hotel lot. There would be no workouts tonight; everyone was tired despite the rush of adrenaline from the day's events. As the family headed into the lobby, the woman at the desk recognized them and motioned for them to come over.

"Good evening. The Arlingtons, right?" she asked in a quiet voice.

"That's correct," Mrs. Arlington said. "Is there a message or a package for us?" She was expecting an overnight package from her office.

"Well, yes, here's an overnight envelope for you," said the woman. "But there's also a short, stocky man asking to see you, Mrs. Arlington, as soon as you get in. He's been waiting in the snack bar for almost an hour."

Mr. and Mrs. Arlington looked at each other.

"It couldn't be him!" Adam whispered. "The thief?"

Mr. Arlington put his arm around his wife protectively and reached in his pocket for the cell phone.

"I don't know, but I'm not going to take any chances," Mr. Arlington said. "I'm calling Detective Simon and the City of Palmdale police."

The cell phone's batteries had gone dead, so he asked the woman at the desk if he could use her phone.

"Sure, anytime," she said, "but here he comes now with his friend. They're right behind you."

Mr. Arlington whirled around to face the man.

Adam's Golden Dream

As everyone quickly turned around, they did indeed see a short, stocky man. However, to their intense relief, he looked nothing like one of the thieves. He was an older gentleman, perhaps nearing eighty, and the friend with him was Mrs. Edwards.

"You're back!" Mrs. Edwards said, hugging Ashley and Adam. "I was starting to worry about you all."

"Worry about *us?*" said Mrs. Arlington. "Mrs. Edwards, Detective Simon is worried about *you.* Perhaps you should call him; here's the number. I'm sure you can use the phone here at the front desk."

Mrs. Edwards held up her hands to pause Mrs. Arlington. "It's all right, dear, I'm fine. We'll call him. But first, let me introduce you to this kind man, Dr. Henry Holmes. Dr. Henry, these are the Arlingtons, Alex and Anne, and their wonderful children, Ashley and Adam."

They all shook hands.

"Dr. Henry called me this morning and came over from UCLA in Westwood, where he teaches American history," Mrs. Edwards explained. "Professor Anne, I imagine you'll have a lot to say to each other. He enlightened me further on the story of Sutter's Mill. He used to teach up in the Bay Area, and he retired to this area. But UCLA offered him a year's position as fill-in head of the history department, though he's just a little past retirement age." She smiled at Dr. Holmes, who also laughed. "He decided to give it a go at UCLA before retiring for good. He heard about our sawmill story on the news and wanted to make contact with me. He's been sharing his thoughts on my missing saw blade and on the other equipment I have left."

The Arlingtons looked at each other.

"We have some thoughts to share, too; boy, do we!" said Adam. He filled in Mrs. Edwards and Dr. Holmes on the day's events and the sighting of the thieves in Barstow.

"What an amazing development!" Mrs. Edwards said. "We were just having coffee in the hotel's restaurant while we waited for you. Would you all like to join us and tell us more?"

Mr. and Mrs. Arlington both agreed. Mrs. Arlington couldn't wait to visit with a fellow colleague and learn what they were doing and share her work. Adam and Ashley, although they enjoyed history thanks to their mother, knew that it was going to be "professor talk" about students and curriculum, so they said good night to the adults and headed up to their suite.

"It's great to see you again, Mrs. Edwards, and nice to meet you, Dr. Holmes," Ashley said on their way out. "We'll look forward to seeing you again tomorrow."

Mrs. Edwards called Detective Simon, who was greatly relieved to hear her voice.

"I'm quite all right, Detective, and I have the Arlingtons here to bring me up-to-date on the case. Thank you for working so hard on it. Keep up the fine work, and good night," she told him.

As the group sat talking in the restaurant for over an hour, they discovered Dr. Holmes was a wealth of information about Sutter's Mill and the discovery of gold.

"It's been something that has interested me since I was a small child growing up in northern California," Dr. Holmes said.

"Listening to the stories he has recounted, I felt like I was sitting right there alongside the water, hearing men shout as they uncovered more and more gold by the minute, becoming instantly rich," Mrs. Edwards said. "Imagine such excitement at a time when California was almost completely barren of settlements and people. That didn't last long after the Gold Rush, did it, Dr. Henry?"

"No indeed," Dr. Holmes agreed. "And speaking of development, I must be on my way. I have to prepare some notes for an eight o'clock class tomorrow morning. But with all the fun of meeting Mrs. Edwards today, I am energized with new inspiration to enlighten all those young minds at school," he smiled. "I'd best take Esther home as well. Perhaps she'll tell me more about her ancestor's Gold Rush involvement."

"Wonderful!" said Mrs. Arlington. "What a good idea. But you two had better call it a night with an early class like that—I can certainly relate to those early mornings!"

After Dr. Holmes's car pulled away, the Arlingtons went up to their suite and found the teens already fast asleep.

But Adam's book of General Sherman's memoirs was still open, and the kids had also printed out several pages from the Internet about the Gold Rush.

"Looks like they take after you, Professor Anne," Mr. Arlington said, thumbing through a few of the pages, then hugging his wife.

"They take after you as well—I wouldn't be surprised if one or both turn out to be criminal investigators or lawyers," she said.

"Right, one will apprehend the thieves, and the other will prosecute them for the district attorney's office," he laughed. "They'd make a great team."

"They already do," Mrs. Arlington said. "Criminals, watch out! I wonder what's going through their minds right now? The last few days have been a whirlwind of history and high excitement."

Adam woke up and saw his parents. "Done already?" he asked. "Wow, it's only 10:00 and Ash and I were out cold. We must've been even more tired than we thought."

Mrs. Arlington went over and gave him a hug. "Lots of excitement and mental energy have been flowing," she said. "It's no wonder you're tired. So are we."

Both parents wished Adam good night, then headed upstairs to their bedroom.

Adam smiled to himself. There had been a lot to digest on this trip, no doubt about it. He picked up Sherman's memoirs and started to read again, but he only made it through a couple of pages before drifting off again.

"Adam! Adam!" a voice called out.

The dust was swirling, and Adam could feel the dirt in his mouth. He took off his cowboy hat and reached down into the stream, scooping up a handful of water and splashing it on his face. There was a flurry of activity upriver. Hands flew in the air and voices shrilled, which could only mean one thing: more gold. Several miners around him headed that way, but Adam stayed put. He reached down and panned through the dirt, going deep into the stream with both hands.

Three shiny objects caught his attention. He quietly pulled them out and looked at them, studying them carefully.

Yep, another three nuggets, he said to himself, smiling. *Now I can buy that parcel of land south of here, build my home, and raise a family.* The sky was blue, the sun resting high in it. It was a glorious day in more ways than one, Adam thought.

Suddenly he felt something hit him sharply in the thigh.

Claim jumpers! his mind screamed. He broke out in a cold sweat, adrenaline pumping through his body.

They're here to steal my gold—my dreams!

Then he heard a heavy thud. That woke Adam up. It was his book, which had slipped down his chest and hit him on the thigh before falling to the floor with a thud.

Oh well, who knows if it was really gold anyway, Adam chuckled to himself. *But it sure would have been fun to be there and find out—minus the claim jumpers.*

Minivan Mayhem

When Adam and Ashley woke up the next morning, their parents were still asleep.

"Let's slip out and run a couple miles, then grab some fruit and bagels downstairs to bring up to Mom and Dad," Ashley suggested.

Though only 6:30, it was warming up nicely outside. The kids agreed to add another mile after they had already run three. Afterwards, they walked around the hotel parking lot, cooling down their muscles.

"I didn't think I'd have much energy this morning after working so hard in my dream, but that felt great," said Adam.

"I wish *that* dream would come true—except the last part, of course," Ashley told him. "We could be rich!"

Back inside, Adam grabbed two plates of food in the lobby, and Ashley picked up copies of the local paper, the *Antelope Valley Daily Press,* and also *USA Today.* They entered their suite to find their parents still sleeping.

"Rise and shine," Ashley announced, opening the curtains in their parents' bedroom. "It's almost 7:30, and we've got the morning news and breakfast."

"Turn off the light!" Mr. Arlington pleaded jokingly, pulling the covers up over his head as Adam tried to wrestle them away.

Mrs. Arlington sat up. "I think we should go for a morning run," she said.

"You're too late," said Ashley, pointing to her sweaty head. "Think I woke up looking like this? We did four miles already, then walked half a mile to cool down."

Mr. Arlington finally relented and sat up, accepting some bagels and fruit, as did his wife.

"Your mother and I talked last night, and we really need to fill you in on some things," he told the kids.

"What's up?" Ashley asked as she sat next to Adam on their bed.

"You know what today is, right?" Mrs. Arlington asked.

"June 19," Ashley answered.

"Exactly." Mrs. Arlington stood up and fastened her robe. "We're still planning on heading home on June 20, tomorrow. We have plans in Las Vegas on our way through, and then we all have to be home because we have commitments and your father has to get back to his office."

The teens sported looks of disappointment, but this news wasn't unexpected. It seemed like they were never ready to end their vacations—something always came up to grab their interest and make them want to stay longer.

"That's just the way it is, and we understand," sighed Adam. Ashley sighed with him. "We wanted to see this thing through with the sawmill blade," he went on. "If by chance it unfolds today or tomorrow, we'll go ahead and learn what we can. If not, we've still had a great adventure and learned a lot about the history of the California Gold Rush."

"Agreed!" Ashley said. "We'll at least take home our good memories from my play, *Gold Rush Girl,* and our sports camps. And meeting Mrs. Edwards and Detective Simon during the search for the saw blade has given us some great new friends."

Mr. Arlington opened his eyes wide. "You two certainly took that well," he said. "We had a long speech prepared about honoring commitments back home and respecting other people's responsibilities."

Adam grabbed a pillow from the bed and smacked his father on the head.

"You can save that speech for our next trip," Adam said as everyone laughed.

The family ate everything on the plates, then showered and dressed for the day. Mrs. Arlington called Detective Simon first thing, but he had nothing new to report. The green truck yielded few clues, and the police were of the same mind as the Arlingtons, that the thieves had no idea what they had on their hands or what to do with it next.

"They're probably pretty surprised they're being tracked this heavily," Simon told Mrs. Arlington. "They may not have even opened up the case that has the saw blade in it yet. According to the historical society, a case like that is likely welded shut. They'd need to get a welder to open it, and I doubt they want to take that chance now. They know we're hot on their trail and have put messages out to every welder from Los Angeles to Las Vegas to be on the lookout for this thing."

Next Mrs. Arlington called Mrs. Edwards, who invited the family out to her house.

"That sounds good," Mrs. Arlington told her. "We'll do some shopping and get out there around noon, if that's all right."

"Wonderful, dear," Mrs. Edwards said. "I'll have lunch ready."

"No, don't do that. Do you have a grill?" Mrs. Arlington asked.

"Why, yes, I certainly do," Mrs. Edwards replied. "I picked it up new a few years back but haven't used it, so it's brand-new. What do you have in mind?"

"Please let us go to the grocery store and pick up burgers, hot dogs, and all the fixings. We'll barbecue," Mrs. Arlington suggested. "We're leaving tomorrow, and we'd like to have one good sit-down meal with you before we head out."

"I'm looking forward to seeing you, Professor Anne. I may be tending a few of my plants in the backyard, so if I don't answer the door, don't call Detective Simon and report me missing—come on around to the back," Mrs. Edwards instructed.

Mrs. Arlington laughed. "We won't get alarmed this time, then," she said. "We'll see you soon."

After a trip to the mall, the family again stopped at the kids' favorite shopping locale, a bookstore. Ashley and Adam each picked out books on the Gold Rush to read on the long drive home. Adam was a couple dollars short, and Ashley offered to loan him the money.

"Wait a minute," their dad said. "These books are courtesy of your mother and I. You two have been terrific on this trip, and we appreciate it."

"Thanks, Mom and Dad," the kids said in unison.

They made the drive toward the northernmost part of Lancaster.

"You know, the desert is really beautiful out here," Ashley observed.

"It is that," Mr. Arlington agreed. He pointed out the town of Mojave, just north of Rosamond. Mojave was next to Edwards Air Force Base.

"The dry lake beds at Edwards AFB are where the space shuttle has landed in the past when the weather at Cape Canaveral in Florida hasn't been good enough for a landing," he pointed out. "Now that would be a spectacular sight to witness, a shuttle landing on one of these gigantic lake beds!"

The Arlingtons had the route to Mrs. Edwards's house memorized by now. Mr. Arlington prepared for the turn onto the long dirt road that led to the house, but he paused at the stop sign and waited to see what was generating the huge cloud of dust up by her driveway.

"It's a van, one that's going way too fast!" Mrs. Arlington said in dismay.

The dust cloud behind the van was incredibly thick. As the vehicle sped down the hill, Mrs. Arlington recognized it.

"That's the minivan I saw in the college's parking lot in Barstow!" she exclaimed. "Quick, get the cell phone out—we need to call Detective Simon."

"First I need to back up," her husband said, looking over his shoulder to make sure no cars were behind them. "These guys must be going at least 70 miles an hour, maybe faster. They're either going to take this corner way too fast and risk hitting us or just blow through the stop sign right in front of us. Either way, that van is way out of control." He backed up quite far and then handed his wife the cell phone.

Within a couple seconds, the minivan went flying by them. Mrs. Arlington barely made out the face of the driver, but she saw that both of the thieves were in the front seat, and both were wearing hats. The cloud of dust made visibility almost zero for a moment.

"Mrs. Edwards! Quick, Dad, head up the road—we have to see if she's all right!"

"We'll get to her as quickly as we can, but let's be careful," Mr. Arlington said. "We have to let the dust settle a little. What if a police cruiser comes zipping down here chasing that van? It could slam into us. Maybe that's why they're going so fast."

As the dust started to settle, Mr. Arlington saw there were no other cars in sight. He could see Mrs. Edwards's house now, and to the family's great relief, she came hurrying around the side of it. He pulled carefully down the road and into her driveway.

Mrs. Arlington was on the phone with Detective Simon as they pulled in, telling him where they were and what they had seen.

"I'll alert the police and sheriff's offices, and then I'll head out there, too!" Simon said.

She hung up the phone and rolled down her window. "Are you all right?" she yelled to Mrs. Edwards, who was wearing gardening gloves and a big straw hat to keep off the sun.

"Oh, yes, dear," Mrs. Edwards said calmly, not nearly as perturbed as the Arlingtons were. "Why, I heard a car out here in the driveway, and at first I thought it was you. It came up by the garage, I heard a door slam, and by the time I peered around the corner, it was already kicking up dirt and speeding away. But then, here you are after all. Oh, my," she hesitated, suddenly paling and leaning against the side of the house for support. "You don't think that was the thieves again, coming back for more of my collection?"

"We've already called Detective Simon, and he's on his way to check into it. Let's go inside and get you a drink of water," Mrs. Arlington told her, getting out of the SUV and running to give the elderly woman her arm.

Adam and the rest of the family got out, too. He noticed something by the garage, in a patch of landscaped bushes.

"Look," he exclaimed. "There's something over there in the brush. Was that there before, Mrs. Edwards?"

Mrs. Edwards looked where he was pointing. "Honey, I can't see that far," she said. "We better take a look before we go in."

Ashley took Mrs. Edwards's other arm, and Adam and Mr. Arlington led the way across the drive to the side of the garage. As they got closer, Mrs. Edwards stopped.

"Why, that's definitely the sawmill blade's cast-iron case—can you believe it?" she said, leaning heavily on Mrs. Arlington and Ashley in her surprise.

Adam looked for openings, but didn't notice any. "It still looks sealed, very solidly," he reported. He reached out to touch it, but his father stopped his hand.

"Hey, Son, we better wait till the police get here," Mr. Arlington said.

"Good thinking, Dad; you're right," Adam agreed sheepishly. "I'm just so curious about what the blade looks like inside it. That thing looks like it's been sealed forever, kind of like a minivault."

Mrs. Arlington looked back toward the SUV. "Not that I'm itching for a burger just this minute, Esther, but would it be all right if I took everything inside and put the meat in your refrigerator?" she asked.

"By all means, and I'll go with you," Mrs. Edwards answered. "I could use that glass of water now."

Ashley and her mother helped Mrs. Edwards to a chair in her kitchen, then Ashley went back outside to get the food from their car while her mother got ice water for Mrs. Edwards.

"So those guys just came up the road, slid to a stop by the garage, tossed the case out, and blazed away?" Ashley asked her dad, who was waiting outside with Adam for the police.

"Looks that way," he answered, handing her the grocery bags from the car. "Tell Mrs. Edwards she should be prepared to answer as much as she can about what happened. I'm sure the police will want to hear everything she can remember."

"Okay, Dad," Ashley said, carrying the bags inside.

"The whole thing couldn't have taken more than fifteen seconds," Mrs. Edwards was saying when Ashley walked in. "Certainly I don't move as fast as I once did. By the time I heard the car, got up off my knees, and turned the corner of the house, they were hightailing it down the road. When the dust cleared, I saw you all. I'm just glad you're all right."

"And we're glad you're all right, too," Ashley said, putting her arm around Mrs. Edwards. "Dad says to be prepared to answer questions again. The police will probably want to hear everything you just told us."

A county sheriff's car came up the driveway, closely followed by Detective Simon's car.

"Everyone okay?" Simon asked, coming into the kitchen.

"Oh, yes," Mrs. Edwards assured him. "Just a little surprised." She recounted her story about the minivan speeding up the road and into her driveway, pushing the cast-iron case—which presumably still had the saw blade inside it—into the bushes, and squealing off.

"Odd! But if they were trying to get off the hook by returning your stolen property, it won't work. We've got them this time! I heard a report as I pulled in that a pair of police cruisers is following close behind, and if these guys try to head out of the county, we've got the helicopter on the way. They're not going anywhere this time. Not today."

Mr. Arlington and Adam walked into the kitchen, accompanied by a young deputy who was first on the scene, Rob Connor.

"Detective Simon? Sir, they have the suspects in custody about nine miles down the road, just within the Palmdale city limits," he reported.

"Yes!" Adam yelled.

"This is great!" Ashley said, smiling.

"I love a happy ending," Mrs. Edwards said, taking Mr. and Mrs. Arlington's hands in hers.

"But . . . what about the cast-iron case—I mean, what now?" Adam asked.

Cracking the Case

Detective Simon and Deputy Connor exchanged looks. "I don't think that cast-iron case would bode well for fingerprinting, and we have plenty of eyewitnesses who saw that van drop the case here anyway," Connor said.

"Then I'd say the next move is up to you, Esther," Detective Simon said.

"My goodness, hmmm," she said, rubbing her hand on her chin. "I think it would be nice if we could have someone come out here and—open it!"

Everyone cheered.

Connor had an idea. "Detective Simon, I could call the county garage and have a welder out here within an hour or two if you'd like," he said.

"Great; go ahead," Simon said appreciatively.

"Should we also contact the media?" Connor asked.

"They're already on it with the police scanners, and no

doubt they'll show up here anyway—might as well be invited and organized as not, before it becomes a circus around here."

"Good point," Simon said. "But again, I defer that decision to you, Mrs. Edwards."

She thought about it a moment. "That would be nice," she decided. "We didn't get to have the big 'grand opening' event like we planned before, so we can have it today. Why don't you tell them to meet here in about ninety minutes? I know this is very exciting for everyone, most of all me. But I have to be honest—I'm really hungry! That would give us time to eat first."

Everyone got a good laugh out of that. Connor waved as he headed out the door to wrap things up outside.

"Detective Simon, we were planning on having a big barbecue out back today anyway before all this excitement. Will you stay and have burgers and hot dogs with us?" Mrs. Edwards asked.

"I'd love to," Simon said. "But can we do it out front? We need to keep an eye on that case this time. After all this, I'd rather it wasn't out of sight," he grinned.

Everyone chuckled again as they went outside. Mr. Arlington and Adam carried the picnic table around front, and Mrs. Arlington and Ashley did the same with the grill.

Detective Simon was back by the garage, kneeling alongside the cast-iron case. "This thing must weigh 200 pounds," he called. "Those two thieves were probably glad to have it off their hands. I'm a little surprised they brought it back here, though. Why not just dump it at the side of the road? You'd think they could reason out that they'd probably get caught by returning to the scene of the crime!"

Adam and Ashley manned the grill while their parents helped Mrs. Edwards bring out the chips and two huge containers of homemade lemonade.

"You think that cast-iron case has secrets in it? Well then, you just ought to taste my lemonade," Mrs. Edwards said, luring Detective Simon over to get a glass.

He smiled and thanked her, then picked up a burger. Just as he finished it, his cell phone rang. He picked it up and listened for what seemed like fifteen minutes, occasionally interrupting to ask a question. "Good work," he finally said to the deputy he had been talking with, then he closed his phone. "The guys who stole your case have been interrogated and have confessed to their crime," he told Mrs. Edwards.

"Why did they do it?" Adam asked curiously.

"They heard about it on the radio, found Mrs. Edwards's address in the phone book, and thought they could make a few easy bucks taking it to Vegas," Simon said. "Turns out they were a little overwhelmed by it—the taller guy actually has some sort of abdominal injury from picking it up the night they stole it. Things kind of unraveled for them the night Ashley spotted them at the hotel. From then on they were on the run. They had slept in the truck during the day in the desert—which must have left them feeling just plain baked. And they traveled to Barstow at night."

"So once they got to Barstow, they ditched the pickup truck?" Ashley asked this time.

"Exactly; stole a minivan from a used car lot and put the truck's plate on it," Simon explained. "But since you spotted the van at the college, Anne, we were tipped off again as to their whereabouts. They had decided by then that they had to know exactly what it was they were lugging around and risking life imprisonment over. They went to the college to see if they could find out. They had no luck there, either. The short, stocky guy said they heard the sirens as they left the college, so they went into the desert again southwest of Barstow. They were going to dump the thing in the desert."

"Why didn't they?" Mrs. Arlington asked.

"They were tired of being on the run, and they realized they weren't getting anywhere," Simon said. "For some reason they had a burst of conscience and decided to return the case here. One of them had a grandmother who was fond of her antiques—I suppose they figured if they weren't going to get anything out of the relic, Mrs. Edwards might as well have it back in her possession. They said they would never have harmed her—that's something anyway, not that it will do them any good with the 'three-strikes' law in effect. But at least the one had a real affection for his grandmother, and it carried over into a respect for the elderly—which probably saved you from personal injury, Esther."

"Bless the woman," Mrs. Edwards said with a tear in her eye. "She must have been a good influence. It's a shame her grandson still turned to a life of crime."

"It sure is," Simon agreed. "After they dumped the case here," he went on, "they planned to ditch the minivan and go their separate ways, their idea being to get out of state as soon as possible, maybe even go to Mexico and reconnect there. They hoped the search for them would die down after everyone realized they had returned the sawmill blade."

"So will they get off any easier for returning it?" Adam asked.

"Hardly," his dad answered, his lawyer's mind thinking ahead. "That may have been taken into consideration prior to sentencing if this was a first offense, but with their two prior felony convictions already against them, it won't matter. As I understand California state law, their ball game is over—three strikes, and they're out for good." He looked at Simon, who nodded.

"Right, and even if that weren't the case here, they're still facing two counts of felony vehicle theft, property theft, evading arrest, reckless driving, and a few other charges I can think of," Simon pointed out. "At least one had a decent bone in his body, though, and they returned the case here."

A parade of two police cruisers, a couple television news media trucks, and a sheriff's SUV came up the hill toward the driveway. After several minutes of introductions all around, Detective Simon led Mrs. Edwards over to the cast-iron case. The cameras started rolling.

"Mrs. Edwards, I would like to ask your permission for our welder to open this Sutter's Mill saw blade case left to you by your ancestor, Arnold Atkinson," Simon said.

"I'd appreciate that very much," she answered.

"I'd like everyone to back up quite a bit," cautioned the welder, Derek Munson. "And please don't look at the flame on my torch, because it could hurt your eyes." He inspected the case thoroughly, and with help from Simon and a couple deputies, positioned the case more upright.

"Remember, we're pretty certain there's a saw blade in there," Simon said to Munson. "And while we don't know for sure, it could still be very sharp. Take precautions if it opens unexpectedly as you get going—you don't want it to fall to the side and hit you. It would cause you to have to get one whale of a tetanus shot!"

Munson lowered his visor, and Simon and the deputies backed up. A photographer from the *Antelope Valley Daily Press* positioned himself to get photos of the event, and the TV crews zoomed in their cameras for a close-up.

Munson started on one side, then shifted to the other. "I'm going to try to get both sides just loose enough so we can pull them off," he said. "That should prevent whatever's inside from being damaged by the torch."

"Honey, that thing has survived 150 years already and was dumped here by a speeding vehicle today, but I appreciate you doing whatever you can to take the best care of it," Mrs. Edwards said.

The crowd laughed at her comments.

A reporter from the *Daily Press* made some notes in his notebook and walked over to Ashley and Adam. "I'd like to interview you two after a while, if it's all right with your parents," said the reporter, Phil Langlin.

Mr. and Mrs. Arlington agreed that would be fine. Langlin also asked Mrs. Edwards for an interview, who said she'd gladly spend as much time with him as he needed after the "grand opening," as she called it, was over.

Munson shut down his flame and motioned for Simon and the two deputies to join him.

"The cast iron is very hot where I did the cutting," he said. "We need to shift it again—this thing is more secure than a safe! Getting the sides loose enough to pull apart isn't easy. From this opening I've made, you can see where the blade is, though."

He pointed inside, and Simon crouched to take a better look. The camera crews and photographers also asked permission to film through the opening before Munson continued. Mrs. Edwards herself took the final peek inside, then Munson had them all step away.

"I'm going to work on the other side, farthest from where the blade is resting," he informed them. "I'll need a few minutes more, and that should do it." Pulling down his visor and firing up the torch, he went back to work.

"This is so exciting!" Ashley said to Adam and Mrs. Edwards.

Mrs. Edwards was almost trembling with excitement. "This is more suspense than this poor old heart has had to put up with in a long time!" she said.

Mr. Arlington brought her a lawn chair, and Mrs. Arlington handed her a cool glass of lemonade.

"Thank you, dears," she said. "I don't like the circumstances around the theft that brought us all here today, but I sure am glad you're here and that I've met you. Truthfully, I'll be kind of sad to see this end! But it will be marvelous to finally get some answers."

Munson turned down the control on his blowtorch, extinguishing the flame. Mr. Arlington handed him a glass of lemonade, and he drank deeply.

"My work is complete," he said. A cheer went up from the onlookers. They all surged forward, but he held out his hands. "Wait a minute, we need to take a couple of minutes to let the metal cool down," he explained. "It's like a teakettle that's been on the stove a little too long, so I'd wait a few minutes to touch it."

Just then another car drove up containing two members of the California Historical Society, Margaret Jackson and Ted Brown. Behind it came an SUV with Henry Holmes at the wheel, much to Mrs. Edwards's delight.

"What an ever so pleasant surprise!" Mrs. Edwards approached him as he got out of his car. He took her hand. "Ashley," Mrs. Edwards said, "could I persuade you to get Dr. Henry a glass of my freshly made lemonade?"

Dr. Holmes explained that he was acquainted with the historical society members who were on hand. "When they called and asked if I would like to observe the opening of the case with them, I was elated," Holmes said. "Of course, they were quite astonished to learn that I had just been visiting Mrs. Edwards up here the day before."

Ashley and Adam smiled at each other. Dr. Holmes and Mrs. Edwards obviously enjoyed each other's company. Adam went with Ashley to get the lemonade.

"Would you check out the case, Derek, and see if you can give us the green light?" Simon said to Munson.

"Sure. Let's get a couple of tarps out of my car and put them underneath it so we don't lose anything that might fall out of the case," Munson suggested.

The two deputies had heard Munson's idea and gone to get the tarp. They spread it out under the case. Munson felt the case first with his thick, protective gloves. Then he took the gloves off and touched it with his bare hands.

"It's fine now," he said. "Have at it."

"Mrs. Edwards, come on up here," Simon said, smiling.

"Let me have Adam and Ashley Arlington come too. Mr. Munson had you and the deputies help him, and he's younger than me. I might need assistants, too, at my age."

The crowd clapped as the teens joined Mrs. Edwards around the case.

"We'll all need to help with it since it's so heavy," Simon assured her. "How about if you stand on one side, while I stand on the other?" he asked Mrs. Edwards. "Derek, you and the deputies stand behind the case and support it from the backside, while Adam, Ashley, Mrs. Edwards, and I try to roll the front side of the case out of the way. Mrs. Edwards, kids, roll it my way."

On Simon's count of three, they all pushed the front side toward him, while he pulled.

"It opened right up, like cracking a nut!" Adam said.

"Exactly," Munson said. "It's like two halves of a walnut shell, and the saw blade is the nut."

"And we're like busy squirrels trying to get to our prize inside the shell!" Mrs. Edwards laughed.

"All right," Simon said, "let's lean it back so the backside comes to rest on the ground."

As Munson and the deputies tipped their half backward and the kids and Mrs. Edwards stepped out of the way, the crowd got their first glimpse of what was inside. There were cries of amazement as the saw blade was revealed. It looked a good three feet in circumference, with sharp teeth. There was a huge gash visible and a shiny rock embedded deeply in the teeth. Perhaps a dozen teeth were missing around the rock, and the rock appeared to have melted part of the blade, which had allowed the rock to remain so firmly stuck after all the time and travel the case had been through.

"Wow!" Adam called out, always the expressive one.

Dr. Holmes came forward and looked more closely at the case on the ground. "There's gold dust all over the inside of this," he announced. Kneeling down, he took another look. "There's also gold dust all over the saw blade. And yes, to answer the question that has to be running through every head right now, this is a big—in fact, a *very* big—gold nugget stuck within the blade."

The Arlingtons and the rest of the onlookers started clapping, and the media moved in to get better shots. Mrs. Edwards bent down, with Dr. Holmes assisting her.

"My goodness," she said, "this is a huge blade. And the teeth are so sharp. Can I touch the gold nugget?"

"Very carefully," Holmes answered, taking her hand and directing it around the sharp teeth to the gold. She was moved to tears as she finally touched the relic, and one ran down her cheek. But at the same time she was smiling.

"I'm so thankful to you kids, and all of you, for making this day happen," she said.

"Dr. Holmes, would it harm the blade to take it out of the casing and put it down on the tarp for a better view?" Mr. Arlington asked.

"No, I don't think so," Holmes answered slowly. "It's not fastened in with anything, although the casing was very tight front and back—that's probably why the blade is still in such good shape."

Simon, Munson, and Mr. Arlington lifted the blade gently out of the casing. The three were relieved that it was much lighter by itself than it had been when combined with its case.

Everyone's eyes were on the blade and the huge gold nugget gleaming in the sunlight, but Ashley turned to look again at the backside of the case it had been lifted out of.

"Wait a minute—what's that?" she wondered aloud, drawing in a quick breath. All eyes turned her way.

In the bottom half of the case, packed away probably 150 years before, was a worn leather pouch.

A Second "Grand Opening"

"What could it be?" Adam asked in surprise.

The pouch was in good shape, though weathered. It was closed with what appeared to be a leather strip sewn all the way around, and it was no bigger than a legal-sized mailing envelope.

Holmes picked up the pouch and handed it to Mrs. Edwards.

"Could someone help me open this?" she asked.

"I have a pocket knife," Simon offered, taking the pouch from her and surveying how best to open it. "I don't want to damage this, Mrs. Edwards," he said after a minute. "It may contain a valuable piece of history, but I'm afraid if I cut the stitching, we won't ever be able to restitch it in just this way again. What would you like me to do?"

Mrs. Edwards thought about it for a moment. "Well, Detective Simon, it's been a century and a half since it was closed, so I think it's time we opened it again—even if it means it has to stay open forever. We can only learn from our past if we know what it is, after all," she smiled.

The crowd clapped again, applauding her decision.

Simon carefully cut out a few stitches and unlaced some more with his fingers. The pouch still wouldn't open.

"There's some sort of adhesive that has been used to seal the pouch shut," he said. "I imagine it is whatever they used for glue back in those days."

"It certainly works well, even after 150 years!" Mrs. Edwards laughed. "But go ahead, do what you must to get at the contents—two 'grand openings' in one afternoon is far more excitement than I ever expected!"

Simon slid the small blade of his knife carefully into the glue, just the very tip, and wiggled it. He dragged the blade back and forth a couple inches. Then he folded the knife and put it in his pocket. He eased the pouch open with his fingers while everyone crowded in closely.

"Here you go, Esther," he said. "This is your show. I think there might be a message in here for you."

Mrs. Edwards's hands were shaking. "Kids, would you please help me again?" she asked Ashley and Adam.

She held the pouch in her hands as the teens pulled back the loosened side.

"There's a paper in here, maybe two!" Adam told everyone.

"Be careful, now," Dr. Holmes urged them. "Handle it with great care, because that paper may be extremely brittle. Bending it the wrong way even a little bit could tear it apart or even make whatever's written on it illegible."

"Go ahead, Sis," Adam said, knowing his sister sometimes had a more gentle touch. Ashley pulled up two folded papers, one on top of the other.

"Open them up, kids," Mrs. Edwards said.

Ashley handed the bottom paper to her brother. Just as Dr. Holmes had instructed, Adam and Ashley were extremely careful. Mr. Arlington came over to Ashley to help her unfold her note, while Mrs. Arlington supported Adam's note in her hands as he unfolded it.

"This one is a map!" Ashley cried.

Dr. Holmes looked at it. "It's a map to Sutter's Fort," he said, putting on his reading glasses. "It has the routes various groups took to get to the area where the fort and lumber mill were being built."

The map was made of small drawings done in black ink, and many of the letters were not easy to make out.

"It says here 'gold discovered,' and it has a little arrow pointing to the place," Holmes noted. "If you'd like, Esther, we could take this to the laboratory at UCLA where I have a microscope and other instruments we could use to decipher the rest of it."

Adam now had his paper unfolded. The letters on his page were large, unlike the map's letters, but there were few of them. They read:

> This gold nugget wrecked this blade in the middle of a busy time at the mill. The gold had settled into a piece of wood, and we never saw it, even though we always cleaned the wood very thoroughly before we ran it through the mill. I showed this to Captain Sutter, and he threw his hands up in the air. "This gold will lead to my

demise. I just know it!" Sutter proclaimed to me, the rage in his heart causing his face to turn red. To Captain Sutter, the gold seems more a curse than a blessing, though other men are quickly making their fortunes from it. I can't help being hopeful along that vein myself.... Perhaps this case and its contents can serve as a token so folks who come here in the late 1800s and maybe beyond can use it to understand the gold fever that's encompassing everything and everyone here now.

Adam was stunned.

"Is it signed?" Ashley asked.

Adam glanced down the final fold. "It is," he said. "It reads 'Lt. A. Atkinson,' and it's dated, well, it's hard to make out." He handed the note to Dr. Holmes.

"It is dated June 19, 1848," Holmes said after scrutinizing it carefully a minute or two. "If my watch date is correct, that would be the same date as today, June 19, 2001."

"One hundred and fifty-three years to the day!" Ashley exclaimed. "Incredible!"

Mrs. Edwards was overwhelmed. "That would be written by Arnold Atkinson, my blood relative!" she said proudly. "This is all so much for me to take in," she said, wavering a little. "It's very hot out here, and I'd like to retreat to my living room now, if that's all right. Detective Simon, could you and the Arlington kids make sure the blade and its case are taken care of? I'll take the notes into the house, if you'll help me, Henry."

Dr. Holmes escorted Mrs. Edwards into the house with the letter, map, and pouch. The media interviewed the

Arlingtons and Detective Simon outside, then they went into the house a few at a time to wrap up their stories with Mrs. Edwards. By the time the press, Derek Munson, and the media headed to their cars, the sun was going down.

"Nice out here now, isn't it?" Mrs. Edwards said to Detective Simon, bringing out fresh refills of lemonade for him and for herself.

"Nice indeed, and much more peaceful," he laughed. He looked toward the garage. "I wonder how many other pieces of history you have in there?" he said. "I hope they don't all cause as much of an uproar as the saw blade did."

It was her turn to laugh at that.

"We're not going to be needing the case or its contents for evidence; my deputies have taken pictures of everything," he told her. "But if you'll tell me that we can have access to it if need be for court proceedings, I can certainly leave it in your care."

"Of course access is yours anytime," she said, "but I hope you'll come out my way to visit even if you don't need further evidence!"

"Your secret recipe lemonade would make it worth my trip," he said. "Will you be leaving its recipe to posterity sealed inside a metal lemonade pitcher? I think you should!"

Dr. Holmes came out of the house just in time to second that opinion. "It would be a shame for this recipe to be lost for all time!" he said, holding up his own emptied glass. He once again studied the saw blade. "I would venture that the gold within that would be worth a good bit of cash, not to mention the value of the blade itself and even the cast-iron case. I warrant that case itself has a quite interesting story behind it, if we only knew . . ."

"In this day alone I've had enough interesting stories to last the rest of my life, however long that may be," Mrs. Edwards chuckled.

That elicited smiles from the Arlingtons and Dr. Holmes, who, along with Simon and the two officials from the historical society, were the only ones left on the property.

"So may I ask what you'll do with these now?" Ashley asked.

"My dear, I couldn't answer that when all those reporters were questioning me, but I can answer it for you," Mrs. Edwards said as she took Ashley's hand. "I've been doing some thinking since they all left. Did you see the look on everybody's faces when that case was opened? Their eyes opened wide, and they looked like they stopped breathing for a second—I know I did. That isn't always a good thing at my age, you know," she laughed. "But what I'd like to do is give that feeling to as many other folks as possible, especially our young people. I'd like for these things to be on display in a museum hereabouts for a month or two, then I'd like them to be on display at an appropriate place up in northern California, as close to Sutter's Fort as possible."

Margaret Jackson and Ted Brown smiled broadly at her announcement.

"It's a great day for the California Historical Society, and a great day for history, too," Dr. Holmes said. "I'll help you with the proper displays and information however I can, Marge and Ted."

Mrs. Edwards decided that Marge and Ted, longtime acquaintances of Henry Holmes, could transport the sawmill blade and its case to a secure area at the museum right away. Simon could look in on them there if he needed to see them again.

"I'll set up a police escort with the highway patrol to get you there safely, and they won't leave you until these are locked up tonight," Detective Simon offered.

The offer was gladly accepted, and the Arlingtons helped load the relics carefully into the back of the historical society's staff vehicle, a large SUV with back doors that opened plenty wide. Holmes helped pack everything in to make sure nothing would shift or be otherwise damaged during the drive to the museum, which was also in Los Angeles County.

The vehicle drove slowly down the dirt road, and everyone waved. Simon said he too had to be on his way. Mrs. Edwards gave him a big hug and wouldn't let him leave till she went into the house and came back out with a huge piece of fresh apple pie wrapped up for him.

"I made this for what was supposed to be a leisurely picnic—which turned out to be anything but that," she laughed.

"You win," Simon said. "I'd be glad to take some pie and enjoy it as I do paperwork late at my office tonight. I promise you it won't go to waste."

"Can you stay and have dessert?" she then asked the Arlingtons.

"We'd love to, except we're heading out early in the morning and really should get back to the hotel to pack," Mrs. Arlington told her.

"Of course, Professor Anne, I understand. Wait right there, though." She went into the house and came back out with the rest of the pie wrapped for the family to take along.

"But Mrs. Edwards, if we take the rest of the pie, what will you and Dr. Holmes have for dessert?" Ashley asked.

"Each other's company," Dr. Holmes answered as Mrs. Edwards blushed a little.

The Arlingtons and Detective Simon said their good-byes.

"I won't forget your kids—or you, Alex and Anne," Simon said. "Let's be honest here: This case wouldn't have been solved so quickly, and perhaps not at all—if not for you four. You gave us the first big clue in the hotel parking lot. Then you found the pickup truck. As if that wasn't enough, you saw the final getaway vehicle, Anne, which allowed us to keep moving in on the thieves. Your sharp powers of observation and concern for Mrs. Edwards, even though you were from out of town, kept pressure on those guys all the way and helped bring this to a happy ending we couldn't have had without you!"

The Arlingtons were grateful for his compliments.

"I think a lot of it was being in the right place at the right time," Mr. Arlington said, extending his hand to shake Simon's. "At the same time, the kids—and my wife— were diligent and paid attention to what was around them. The importance of those two qualities is certainly worth keeping in mind."

"That's what makes a good detective, for certain," Simon said. He promised to keep in touch. "If you kids ever need letters of recommendation for scholarships—or perhaps entrance into the police academy—I want you to contact me without a second thought," he said. "And I know you have my phone number!"

"We do have that—it's burned into our memories by now," Mrs. Arlington called out as he backed down the driveway with a wave.

"I guess this is it, then," Ashley said, hugging Mrs. Edwards. "We're never going to forget you."

Adam also gave her a hug.

"I can promise you won't forget me, because I'll be staying in touch with you and your parents," Mrs. Edwards said, again shedding a few tears.

Mr. and Mrs. Arlington hugged her, and then the family shook hands with Dr. Holmes.

"Mrs. Edwards has our numbers if you ever need to reach us," Mrs. Arlington told him. "And please come be my guest lecturer if you are ever in D.C.!"

"I'll try to work that in," he told her. "I think Detective Simon hit it right on the head about your children. They are special. And while I am retiring at the end of the school year, if I can ever help you in regard to colleges out here, I still have friends at universities up and down the coast, and even nationwide to a degree. You may call me at any time, for any reason."

The Arlingtons got into their SUV, and Dr. Holmes escorted Mrs. Edwards up onto her porch, where they waved at the family as Mr. Arlington backed up the vehicle.

"I know it's too early to tell, but I hope those two get married!" Ashley said.

"Yeah, that would be great," Adam said. "Mrs. Edwards is too nice to be alone, and Dr. Holmes seems like a great guy."

Mr. Arlington rolled his eyes toward his wife.

"What? Alex, don't tell me that thought didn't cross your mind, too!" his wife accused him.

He admitted that it had. Then he told the kids how proud he was of them, and how proud he would continue to be, even if they became matchmakers instead of lawyers or history professors.

"Stop it!" his wife scolded him, elbowing his ribs across the front seat.

"You two did represent yourselves very well," Mrs. Arlington told her kids. "You learned quite a lot about the history of this area, and you helped Mrs. Edwards get her property back by helping the police solve the case," she said. "What did you two get out of this whole adventure?"

Ashley motioned for Adam to go first.

"First of all, I learned that we have to get Mrs. Edwards's recipes for lemonade and apple pie!" Adam said, making his family laugh. "My rewards from this—what I'll really remember—are the people we met and the people we heard about. I mean, come on, Sutter was absolutely devastated to find gold, whereas almost everyone else was jumping up and down about it. He never lost sight of his goal, to be a big lumber supplier. Gold ruined a lot of people, I would guess, because it could act like a drug and corrupt them or change who they were, maybe in a bad way a lot of the time.

"I think it would have been great if Sutter could have overcome the problems that the Gold Rush created for him. Sometimes that's just how life is—we can run into obstacles in the way of anything we do. Who'd have thought the most prized item of the time—gold nuggets—could cause a man so much grief? I guess what I'd apply to my life is to never forget the big picture but to also recognize the value of the little picture. I think Sutter could have figured out a way to work around the gold fever, whether that meant moving his business or taking a break until everything around him settled down. Gold consumed a lot of people, and though it was in a very different way, gold also consumed Captain John Sutter."

"Good points, young man," Mr. Arlington said, reaching his right hand back so Adam could slap him a high five.

Ashley knew it was her turn.

"I learned a lot of the things Adam did, too, but I also developed a belief—or maybe I would call it a theory—on this trip. You can really see how a state's history shapes its personality—that's my theory," Ashley said. "Look at Texas. At the Alamo we saw how a spirit of independence sprang up among the defenders, and that spirit still exists in Texas today. But my theory is especially true in California.

"People came here to chase their dreams. In the mid–1800s, those dreams were to find gold and riches. People still come to California to chase their dreams today, whether they dream of finding 'riches' in the computer country that makes up Silicon Valley, or dream of the shiny kind of gold presented at the Oscars in Hollywood. I mean, how many people come out here every year hoping to make it big as actors, actresses, or movie writers? How many young computer geniuses head this way to chase their dreams of developing the newest and best technology?

"That's the personality of California, what this state is all about, and I think that reputation was born out of the Gold Rush days!" Ashley finished.

"Wow! Well said, Gold Rush Girl!" said her brother. "You sure you want to abandon this golden state and 'begin the long trip home to the East'?"

"Adam!" Ashley exclaimed, playfully slugging her brother in the shoulder.

"Something tells me this *is* going to be a long trip," sighed Mrs. Arlington to her husband as he swerved to avoid a rusty muffler in the road.

California

Fun
Fact
Files

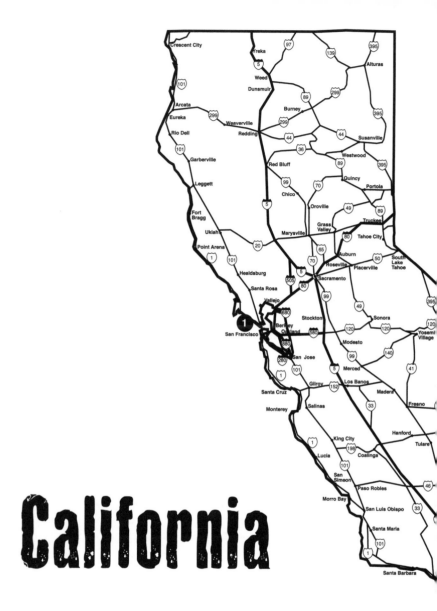

California

The Arlingtons' Route

1. San Francisco
2. Palmdale
3. Lancaster
4. Visalia
5. Barstow

Names and Symbols

Origin of Name:

California was named by the Spanish after the mythical paradise in a Spanish romance written by García Ordóñez de Montalvo in 1510.

Nickname:

The Golden State

Motto:

"Eureka" ("I have found it")

State Symbols:

bird: California valley quail
flower: California poppy
animal: California grizzly bear
song: "I Love You, California"
gemstone: blue diamond
tree: California redwood
fish: California golden trout
mineral: gold

Geography

Location:

Western United States; Pacific coast

Borders:

Arizona (East)

Nevada (East)
Oregon (North)
Mexico (South)
Pacific Ocean (West)

Area:

163,707 square miles (3rd largest state)

Highest Point:

Mount Whitney (14,494 feet) is the highest point in the
lower 48 states

Lowest Point:

Death Valley (282 feet below sea level) is the lowest
point in the United States

Nature

National Forests:

Angeles National Forest
Cleveland National Forest
Eldorado National Forest
Inyo National Forest
Klamath National Forest
Lake Tahoe Basin Management Area
Lassen National Forest
Los Padres National Forest
Mendocino National Forest
Modoc National Forest
Plumas National Forest
San Bernardino National Forest
Sequoia National Forest
Shasta-Trinity National Forest
Sierra National Forest

Six Rivers National Forest
Stanislaus National Forest
Tahoe National Forest

National Parks:

Channel Islands National Park
Death Valley National Park
Joshua Tree National Park
Lassen Volcanic National Park
Mojave National Preserve
Point Reyes National Seashore
Redwood National Parks
Sequoia and Kings Canyon National Parks
Yosemite National Park

Weather

Contrary to popular belief "Sunny California" is not always sunny. Because of its diverse topography, California has four of the five climates found around the world—Mediterranean (relatively warm, dry summers and mild winters), semi-arid, desert, and Alpine (short, cool summers and harsh winters). The only climate not found in California is the hot and rainy tropical climate.

People and Cities

Population:

33,871,648 (2000 census); California is the most populated state

Capital:

Sacramento

Ten Largest Cities (as of 2000):

Los Angeles (3,694,820)
San Diego (11,223,400)
San Jose (894,943)
San Francisco (776,733)
Long Beach (461,522)
Fresno (427,652)
Sacramento (407,018)
Oakland (399,484)
Santa Ana (293,742)
Anaheim (328,014)

Counties:

58

Major Industries

Agriculture:

California's rich soil and long growing season, along with the availability of water for irrigation, make it the country's leading agricultural state. It ranks first in the nation in fruit and vegetable production. Some principal crops are walnuts, nectarines, olives, almonds, lettuce, tomatoes, and broccoli. California also has strong livestock and fisheries industries.

Mining:

Both California's nickname and its motto point to the state's mining heritage. Mining persists as an important part of California's economy today. Crude oil and natural gas are the state's chief products. California is also a leading producer of many minerals, including titanium, clay, talc, salt, copper, silver, and of course gold.

Manufacturing:

California leads the nation in income made from manufacturing. Some of the chief areas of manufacturing are electronics, transportation equipment (such as automobiles, aircraft, and space exploration vehicles), and food processing. California is also a leading manufacturer of computer equipment. Many computer companies are located in what is known as Silicon Valley.

Entertainment and Tourism:

Southern California has dominated the entertainment industry for decades. Hollywood has long been synonymous with the making of motion pictures, and more recently, Los Angeles has become a major center for the television industry. Tourists are drawn to the state's beautiful scenery and big cities. Visitors to California spend more money on lodgings, car rentals, and other travel expenses each year than visitors to any other state.

History

Native Americans:

Prior to the arrival of Europeans, between 100,000 and 150,000 native inhabitants lived in what is now California. Some of the tribes include the Tolowa, Shasta, Modoc, and Kumeyaay tribes. Because California has many different climates and landscapes, native culture varied from region to region. Native tribes were geographically isolated from each other and from other peoples, so their cultures remained essentially the same for thousands of years before the arrival of Europeans.

Exploration and Settlement:

Europeans first set foot in present-day California when Juan Rodriguez Cabrillo explored the Southern coast in 1542 and claimed the area for Spain. In 1579 Sir Francis Drake stopped off at a bay in Northern California during his renowned trip around the world to make repairs to his treasure-laden ship, the Golden Hind. He named the area New Albion and claimed it for England. It was another 200 years before California was actually settled. The Spanish established military bases and missions in California in 1769. Twenty-one missions were established between 1769 and 1823. Besides caring for native souls, the missions were the economic lifeblood of California. They were the area's only source of manufacturing and handicrafts. Workers at the missions tanned hides, made wool, raised wheat and oranges, and made soap, furniture, and leather goods.

In 1811 Mexico revolted and won its independence from Spain. California remained loyal to Spain for a time, but eventually pledged allegiance to Mexico. During the 1840s America's increasing interest in California caused tension with Mexico, and the Mexican War broke out. In 1848 the Treaty of Guadalupe Hidalgo declared California to be a U.S. territory. At the same time gold was discovered. The gold rush brought 80,000 men to California in 1849. The miners were an unruly, energetic, and overly excitable bunch. California was politically and socially unstable. The increase in population required a more effective civil government, and California became a state in 1850.

Statehood:

California entered the union as the 31st state on September 9, 1850.

Check It Out

For more information about the historical people and places in this book, check out the following books and web sites:

California:

Web sites:

http://www.state.ca.us/

http://www.pbs.org/weta/thewest/places/states/california/

http://www.californiahistory.net/

The Gold Rush:

Book:

Ketchum, Liza. The Gold Rush. New York: Little Brown & Co., 1996.

Web sites:

http://www.cagoldrush.com

http://www.goldrush1849.com

http://www.isu.edu/~trinmich/allabout.html

Coloma:

Web site:

http://wiwi.essortment.com/goldrushcoloma_rztz.htm

Gold:

Web site:

http://pubs.usgs.gov/gip/prospect1/goldgip.html

Kit Carson:

Book:

Green, Carl R. and William R. Sandford. Kit Carson: Frontier Scout (Legendary Heroes of the Wild West). Berkeley Heights, N.J.: Enslow Publishers, 1996.

Web site:

http://www.pbs.org/weta/thewest/people/a_c/carson.htm

General William Tecumseh Sherman:

Web sites:

http://www.sfmuseum.org/bio/sherman.html

http://www.pbs.org/weta/thewest/people/s_z/sher man.htm

John Sutter/ Sutter's Mill:

Web sites:

http://www.pbs.org/weta/thewest/people/s_z/sutter.htm

http://www.sfmuseum.org/bio/sutter.html

http://www.germanheritage.com/biographies/mtoz/sut ter.html

General Mariano Vallejo:

Web site:

http://www.pbs.org/weta/thewest/people/s_z/vallejo.htm